# PRA
*Wher*

"W. D. Wetherell can sing in his prose with the best we have. I have long been an admirer of his wide-ranging imaginative journeys through the lives, the heartbreaks, and the courage-in-defeat of his people. His stories are moving and rich with life, they resonate deep down."

—*Richard Bausch*

"Wetherell has written wonderful stories for years. Here are stories that include the American landscape as a crucial character. Here are stories that make you care about how to be good. Here are stories in which nothing less than life and death are at stake. Here is what suspense is about. Here is why you read short fiction."

—*Frederick Busch*

"Wetherell's characters may be losers, but they're battlers, with a cranky dignity that sets them sharply apart from the spoiled whiners, quitters, and self-indulgent identity seekers so frequently encountered in today's fiction."

—*Howard Frank Mosher*

"W. D. Wetherell is an American author of the first order, his work the evidence of his immense literary talent. In his stories, Wetherell combines an effortless elegance and grace of language with a wisdom of the human heart seldom encountered anywhere these days."

—*Brett Lott*

"Wetherell is able to write about the bitterness of life without defeating his characters; in these stories' narrative tone and the narrative stance, in the realism itself, there is a sly, American exaggeration. His characters, like the rest of us, are life's fools, yet when presented this clearly they are almost indistinguishable from angels."

—*Max Apple*

# WHERE WE LIVE

BOOKS BY W. D. WETHERELL

NOVELS:

*Souvenirs* (Random House 1981, New York)
*Chekhov's Sister* (Little Brown 1990, Boston)
*The Wisest Man in America* (University Press of New England
    1995. Hanover)
*Morning* (Pantheon 2001, New York)
*A Century of November* (University of Michigan Press 2002,
    Ann Arbor)
*The Writing on the Wall* (Arcade 2012, New York)

SHORT STORY COLLECTIONS:

*The Man Who Loved Levittown* (University of Pittsburgh Press
    1985, Pittsburgh)
*Hyannis Boat and Other Stories* (Little, Brown 1998, Boston)
*Wherever That Great Heart May Be* (University Press of New
    England 1996, Hanover)
*Hills Like White Hills* (Southern Methodist University Press
    2009, Dallas)

ESSAY COLLECTIONS:

*Vermont River* (Nick Lyons Books 1984, New York)
*Upland Stream* (Little Brown 1991, Boston)
*One River More* (The Lyons Press 1998, New York)
*On Admiration* (Skyhorse Press 2010, New York)
*Summer of the Bass* (Skyhorse Press 2015, New York)
*A River Trilogy* (Skyhorse Press 2017, New York)

MEMOIRS:

*North of Now* (The Lyons Press 1998, New York)
*Yellowstone Autumn* (University of Nebraska Press 2009,
    Lincoln)
*Soccer Dad* (Skyhorse 2008, New York)

TRAVEL/NATURE:

*The Smithsonian Guides to Natural America; Northern New
    England* (Smithsonian Books 1995, Washington, DC)
*Small Mountains* (Terra Nova 2000, Hanover)

CRITICISM/LITERATURE:

*Where Wars Go to Die* (Skyhorse 2016, New York)

FOREIGN EDITIONS:

*Le Soeur De Chekhov* (JC Lattes 1992, Paris)
*Un Siecle de Novembre* (Le Livre de Poche 2008, Paris)
*A Century of November* (Australia Broadcasting Corporation
    Books 2007, Sydney)

# WHERE
# WE LIVE

*stories*

# W. D. Wetherell

GREEN WRITERS PRESS | *Brattleboro, Vermont*

Printed in the United States

10 9 8 7 6 5 4 3 2 1

Green Writers Press is a Vermont-based publisher whose mission is to spread a message of hope and renewal through the words and images we publish. Throughout we will adhere to our commitment to preserving and protecting the natural resources of the earth. To that end, a percentage of our proceeds will be donated to environmental activist groups. Green Writers Press gratefully acknowledges support from individual donors, friends, and readers to help support the environment and our publishing initiative.

*Giving Voice to Writers & Artists Who Will Make the World a Better Place*
Green Writers Press | Brattleboro, Vermont
www.greenwriterspress.com

ISBN: 978-0-9974528-8-4

AUTHOR'S WEBSITE: https://www.wdwetherell.com

COVER: *Cape Cod Morning* by Edward Hopper, courtesy of the Smithsonian American Art Museum. Gift of the Sara Roby Foundation.

COVER & INTERIOR DESIGN: Hannah Wood

PRINTED ON PAPER WITH PULP THAT COMES FROM FSC-CERTIFIED FORESTS, MANAGED FORESTS THAT GUARANTEE RESPONSIBLE ENVIRONMENTAL, SOCIAL, AND ECONOMIC PRACTICES BY LIGHTNING SOURCE. ALL WOOD PRODUCT COMPONENTS USED IN BLACK AND WHITE, STANDARD COLOR OR SELECT COLOR PAPERBACK BOOKS, UTILIZING EITHER CREAM OR WHITE BOOKBLOCK PAPER,, THAT ARE MANUFACTURED IN THE LAVERGNE, TENNESSEE PRODUCTION CENTER ARE SUSTAINABLE FORESTRY INITIATIVE (SFI) CERTIFIED SOURCING.

*For Howard Frank Mosher*

# CONTENTS

Jersey Plates 3

A Friend of Millyard Museum 19

Stars Fell on Alabama 39

Zone of Habitability 55

Call of the Wild 71

Two Chairs 95

The Old Campaigner 117

Day One 135

Assassins 155

# WHERE WE LIVE

# JERSEY PLATES

IT'S A GOOD PLACE FOR A BLUEBERRY STAND, on the road to the national park, with thousands driving past every day, even in September. My sister owns the land—she's planning to put in bumper cars, but in the meantime lets me use it. I buy my berries from Indians up north, load up my pickup, drive down praying the transmission doesn't quit, open the tailgate so it becomes a stand, let Plato out, plant a sign where visibility's good in both directions, slide open my umbrella, shake the night bugs out, wait to see what happens.

I'm the first place you pass that isn't tacky, so that's working in my favor. People hold off on lobsters until they're actually out on the coast, but wild blueberries they can't resist. And if you turn in my lot, stare out the passenger side, you get the first view of the mountains rising up from the sea. The first scent of it, too, at least if the breeze is in the right direction. From the west it carries the smell of French fries and fudge and overheated macadam, but when it's from the east it's all about iodine and balsam and beach grass and kelp.

Mostly it's older folks in September or young families who don't have to worry yet about school. Nice, most of them. Happy to be out here, happy to be buying wild berries, happy to be talking with someone so shabby looking and harmless. Naturally I get assholes mixed in. One-percenters, the entitled, driving big SUVs with Massachusetts or Connecticut plates. They ask if my berries have MSG in them or GMOs or initials I've never heard of, and nine times out of ten leave in a huff after asking the price.

"MSG?" I told one woman who was particularly obnoxious. "Nope, not an ounce. But the Indians pee on them and sometimes they crap."

Their kids can be mean, too. They steal berries from the truck when I'm not looking, go over to where Plato lies sleeping in the shade, try to feed him.

"He doesn't like blueberries," I tell them, pleasantly the first time, not so pleasantly the second.

What's better is when my own kids stop.

"Hey Mr. Shipton!" they'll shout from their rolled-down windows, or "Hey coach!"

I call them my kids, feel very protective, though most of them have already graduated. They get summer jobs in the park waiting tables or cleaning rooms, stay on in the fall, say it's just temporary, but a lot of them come back the next summer and the summer after that, so it's become their life now and they no longer bother slowing down to shout.

The rain put a damper on things last week, but Monday was perfect, and I sold over 60 pints by noon. I was going to shut things down at five, but I still had a few cartons left, and I don't like to disappoint my regulars who get to the coast late and are counting on me to be there.

I'll give it fifteen minutes, I decided. I emptied Plato's water dish, folded up my sign, was heading back to the pickup when a car with Jersey plates pulled in, stopped for a minute near that view I told you about, then continued around to park by the truck.

A woman got out who I guessed was in her late thirties. Attractive, in a quiet, restful kind of way—nothing snobby or fancy. She wore her hair in bangs over her forehead which made me smile because no one wears bangs anymore. She had wide eyes like a girl's, which is unusual, too, since the years usually narrow them. Because it was cool out she had on a baggy pink sweatshirt with MAINE printed across the front. It looked brand-new, so what she must have done, the minute she got to the coast, was stop and buy herself a sweatshirt.

She reached down and scratched Plato's crooked ear, then and only then turned to look at the berries.

"How much are they?" she asked, with that shy smile I mentioned.

*For you, free* I almost said—I only had three pints left. But somehow I sensed that would be the wrong thing to say.

"Four dollars a carton."

She frowned, but just a little.

"Is that a good price?"

"Rock bottom."

We both laughed with that, though it wasn't particularly funny. *Rock bottom.*

She went back to the car for her purse. I wrapped them up in cellophane so they wouldn't roll loose, then gave her the change. And that was it as far as our transaction went. But the interesting thing was that she didn't thank me and leave, but stood there with her eyes even wider than they were before, staring eastward toward the view.

"Your first time up here?"

"My very first time," she said, without turning around. Her next few sentences were meant for the ocean, not me.

"My parents always wanted to visit Maine, but they never did. We went to the Jersey shore in summer, just the three of us. You know—the Jersey shore? They died last winter, both within three weeks, so I thought when my vacation came I'd drive up here for them."

Maybe because she wore no perfume her hair seemed to catch and hold the iodine smell, that salty tang.

"I'm sorry to hear that, about your folks," I said, then, guessing, "Are you a nurse?"

"Same day surgery. Before that I worked in the emergency room."

Plato must have liked the way she scratched his ear, because he limped over now wanting more. She smiled and knelt down beside him.

"You staying in Bar Harbor?" I asked.

"I think just outside it? The Seawall Motel? I found it on line and they had a special."

"Try the brew pub while you're there. It can get pretty rowdy at night, but it's fun. Just promise me not to try their blueberry beer, okay? Anyone who puts berries in beer should be hanged. The bartender used to be one of my students, so make sure you say hi."

"Are you a teacher?"

"Sub. Three days a week. I used to coach basketball, but there are some issues I need to work on, so I don't anymore."

She frowned a little, but not at that.

"But then if you don't like bars, there's a great hike you can go on. The Breakers Trail they call it. It winds through the spruce out to the ocean and it's a great place to watch waves crashing into rocks."

She liked the sound of that—the Breakers Trail. She wrote it down on a little pad, then reached into her carton, took one of the berries out, held it up to the sun like a pearl.

"Blueberries for Sal. My dad used to read it to me and it was always my favorite. What's that sound they make when the berries hit the pail? Kaplook, Kaplite, Kaplint?"

That was funny, her saying that, because the sound in the book is *Kuplink, Kuplank, Kuplunk*. I wondered if I should correct her, then decided against it.

"Your berries are smaller than the kind we have in Jersey. Are they different?"

Not many people ask questions like that or act curious.

"*Vaccinium angustfolium*," I said, showing off. "They grow wild up on the barrens. When the French explorers first landed here they couldn't believe how abundant they were, how delicious. Bluets, they called them, and I think it's a perfect name."

"Bluets?" Saying it made her lips thin and pretty.

I was going to explain more, but a big camper pulled in and I had to go over to help them. I waved for her to wait, but she must have misread it as waving goodbye, because by the time I finished with them she had driven off.

Tuesday was busy, cars kept pulling in, and for a while there was a line winding around Plato to the road. A bike tour stopped and they wolfed down their pints right there and then. A couple in their eighties bought six quarts for canning—you still get them occasionally, old-timers who can fruit for winter. An asshole driving an Audi with his trophy wife gave me a hard time over change. "I only carry hundreds," he said with a smirk, but I told him no problem, counted him out 96 ones in change.

He had New York plates, looked and acted like a stockbroker or hedge fund manager, the lords of creation. You ruined our world, I wanted to say. Bloodsucking leeches, you ruined our world. Anger starts down low in my heels, works itself up through my midsection, boils up through my throat all the time getting hotter and hotter, so I end up wanting to scream just to be rid of all that pressure.

I didn't scream at him though, and the reason I didn't was that I kept thinking about the Jersey plates woman and how serene and quiet she had looked. It calmed me down quite a bit.

She pulled in at the same time she had the day before, just as the shadows softened the heat into a chill. Yesterday her hair had caught the fresh scent off the water, but today it was the light she captured. Her hair seemed blonder than it had the first time, like she was bearing the brightness of the ocean inland.

She held her carton up, her empty green carton.

"They were so good I came back for more."

"You ate a lot."

"Well—the truth is I tripped and dropped them. Going up the steps after I checked in. I'm pretty clumsy sometimes."

She had on the kind of thin sundress someone might wear in Florida, and her arms were all goosebumped. It emphasized the girlish quality I mentioned. Who over the age of 30 ever gets goosebumps?

Plato recognized her and ambled over to be scratched. I wiped the blueberry stains off the tailgate, helped her sit down.

"So," I said, waving my arm toward the east. "How do you like it out there?"

"It's gorgeous. I had no idea. I wrote postcards out on my little balcony, which seemed so strange. I'm always the one who gets postcards, I never send them."

"Drink any blueberry beer?"

She laughed. "I took that hike you recommended—the Breaker's Trail? I was worried the tide might be dangerous, but a ranger told me it was safe for the next three hours, so I got my courage up and went out. It was slippery with seaweed and those rocks are so blocky I had to use my hands for balance, but I never saw anything so beautiful, the way the waves came in and smashed themselves apart."

I nodded. "I like the dignity of it all—the way the waves march in like they're feeling proud and formal right until the very end."

"The only other people out there was this old man with his grandson who must have been five or six. He was really cute—he wore glasses like Harry Potter. He's helping his grandfather across the rocks, I decided, but I had it backwards, because it was the old man helping him. He limped pretty badly—he was handicapped, probably since he was born. But he was so trusting, the way he held his grandfather's hand and looked up at him for encouragement. And they were happy to be out there together watching the breakers. But somehow it got to me, not because it was sad, but because the boy was so trusting. I don't know why, but sitting there on the rocks, my arms wrapped around my legs, I started to sob."

"Yeah," I said, since I didn't know what else to say. A motorcycle pulled in, they took three pints which had to be wrapped extra carefully, and when I came back she was smiling again.

"And then last night I went out for lobster. My first time ever! I wasn't going to go because some restaurants make you feel conspicuous, eating alone, but this place is right out on the docks and no one cares. Thurston's Lobster Pound? It took me forever to eat mine, it seemed so complicated and scary. But I did. Here, look. The waitress took my picture."

"Good for you," I said, staring down. "Your first one? Good for you."

"Her name is Jill Fant. She said she knew you. I told her about the blueberry man out on the highway and she said that was Mr. Shipton who coached her in high school."

"Jill was my point guard, tricky and very smart. She made All-State her senior year. She's waitressing? She promised she was going to try college."

"She said you were everyone's favorite coach. You really took an interest in kids, tried to help them. She said the team went on strike when they let you go."

"Well, that's very nice of her. It wasn't really a strike."

She stared at me closely now, seemed hesitant to probe any further.

"She didn't say anything about college. I asked her what winters were like up here and she put her arms around herself and shuddered."

"They're not so bad," I said quietly.

"Excuse me?"

"You get through them. It's gray, quiet, peaceful. The rocks soften things out on the coast. I know that sounds strange, but they do, especially when the fog coats them in ice. I sub three days usually, Social Studies and English, but some weeks they don't call, so I have lots of time on my hands. There's a cafe out toward the point, Annie's, and I'm a regular. It's built on stilts right over the water. It's me, three or four lobstermen, a couple of ironworkers who are always getting laid off back at the shipyard. We drink our coffees, bitch about the state of the world, tell bad jokes, watch the tide climb the pilings. Boring, right? But it isn't boring. It's some of the best moments of my life, just sitting with them staring out at the fog."

She listened, nodded, finally pointed behind her toward my pints.

"Not many foods are blue."

Like her, I worried I'd gone too far with my mood. "Hey, do me a favor? I need to run to the bank before they close. Can you watch the stand for me?"

"Uh—sure. What do I do?"

"Take people's money. Tell them the berries were picked yesterday, which they were. If you get lonely, there's Plato. But I'll be gone ten minutes."

She was smiling ear-to-ear when I got back, showed me the dollars she had taken in arranged neatly across the tailgate.

"It's so easy! People are so friendly, the berries make them smile. A woman from Texas bought five pints."

It's my fantasy, having someone help me like that. I picture two people sitting there on the tailgate instead of just one, talking about little things while we wait for customers, maybe teasing each other, helping each other out by driving north to get berries while the other stays with the stand. Not a big fantasy. A minor fantasy, the kind that's harmless.

Closing time. I took down the umbrella, helped Plato get in back. It's funny, but I still didn't know her name, and it had gotten to the point where it seemed awkward to ask. Jersey Plates, I called her to myself. Blueberry Man she probably called me.

"I was thinking about trying lobster again tonight," she said, when the shadows finally touched us. "Now that I know how to do it, I mean. Is there any place near here that you like?"

Had she ever asked anyone out before? Had she ever even gone on a date? It was charming, the clumsy way she went about it, and of course I should have stepped in and made it easier. I'm not sure why I didn't. But I didn't need any no's just then, or even their remote possibility.

"Baxter's is even better than Thurston's. It's on the coast road a mile or two further."

"Baxter's?"

"You come back tomorrow and tell me all about it. Promise?"

She didn't answer right away. She took it seriously enough she had to think it through.

"Promise," she finally said. She patted Plato, hopped down from the tailgate, headed over to her car.

"You forgot your berries!" I yelled, but by then she had already driven off.

I didn't feel like going home after that. Bills stuffed in the mailbox, grass waist high, a month's worth of trash. Sometimes instead of facing it, I sleep in the truck, but I wasn't in the mood for that either.

There's a bar back behind Ellsworth the tourists don't know about, and that's where I ended up, though I don't drink anywhere near like I used to. The owner hates the

Red Sox, so you don't have the TV blaring or have to pretend you give a fuck about who's pitching.

I was on my second beer, feeling not particularly good nor especially bad, when I realized I had a problem. It was Tuesday. Tomorrow, Wednesday, was the day I always drove to Machias to get more berries, but if I drove to Machias I wouldn't be there when Jersey Plates came by. I didn't have her cell number, so there was no way to contact her.

I went outside to the parking lot, called Tim Polis who's my supplier. He's hard to get hold of and doesn't say much when you do—it's like he's selling dope, not blueberries— but I convinced him to meet me halfway in two hours with twenty quarts.

He was late getting there, we had an argument over prices, so it was well after midnight by the time I got back. I ended up sleeping in the truck after all, and woke up feeling even shabbier and crankier than usual.

And it was hot again, which may have contributed to what happened. The wind blew from the west, the bad side, and brought the greasy macadam smell that drives me crazy. The day started slow, with only three or four customers— there was construction up the road, and once people got past it they wanted to keep going. But things picked up after that, and once afternoon came I began staring toward the park watching for her Civic.

She came at five just like she had the first two days, and parked in the shade. I had started moving cartons around to make room for her on the tailgate when a car swerved in like the cops were after it, skidding up a cloud of yellow dust.

The Audi again. The stockbroker with his trophy wife. This time they had brought their kid along, with their worst qualities stamped on his face. His father's nose and smirk; his mother's lassitude and self-adoration. He came over to the truck, reached up and swiped some berries, went over to Plato and dropped them in the dirt under his muzzle.

"He doesn't eat berries," I said. "Please move away from him."

He looked like he was going to bawl, that I had scolded him even gently. His mother, who had sat down on the Audi's hood and crossed her legs like a supermodel, made her expression into something meant to be sweet.

"We try to frame things more positively," she said, staring right at me. Then, turning slowly back again, "Jacob? You know dogs don't thrive on a human diet."

Meantime her husband was grabbing pints from the back and lugging them to the car. I wasn't positive, but I was pretty sure he was going to hand me a hundred again and dare me to make change.

Jersey Plates came over now, smiling in that gentle shy way she had, and glad as I was to see her, the timing couldn't have been worse. All I wanted was to be rid of them and have her all to myself so we could talk.

"I have a gift for you," she said, bringing something spoon-shaped from around behind her back.

A piece of driftwood. A beautifully polished piece of driftwood tied with a lacy blue ribbon.

"You found that for me?"

She nodded. "To hold the money down after people pay. I noticed that yesterday when you let me help, how the bills blew away in the wind. I went out on the rocks again and found this where the tide ended."

I was listening to her and keeping one eye out on what

was happening behind me, because things had now taken a turn for the worse.

"Stay right here," I said, putting my arms on her shoulders, giving them a squeeze. "I will be right back."

The kid wasn't just dropping berries in front of Plato anymore but squatting down next to him trying to force them in through his jaws. Plato hated it, but he was too old and stiff to break away, and in any case the kid had his arm rammed down on his back.

"Get away from him," I said. I could feel the heat rising from my heels up through my midsection with nothing to block it from surging higher.

The kid didn't move.

"Get away from him or I'll rip your fucking balls off."

The mother, there on the hood, smiled a smile of supreme ugliness. The father, without changing expression, took his cell phone out and started filming. For evidence probably. He was already thinking of suing.

"You stop, too."

He held the phone out, zoomed in closer. *Make me*, his expression said.

"You're idiots!" I screamed. "Scumbags! There's more integrity in my little finger than you have in all your fat butts. Understand what I'm saying? You and your kind should be exterminated, blown right off this planet. Leeches! Bloodsuckers! Jews! Get the hell out of my sight! Now! Get the hell out or I start shooting!"

I reached into the truck like I had a gun there, but what I grabbed was the last pint of blueberries, hurling them with all my might at the car as it took off. They splattered against the windshield, splattered there like purple bird shit, and I felt good about that, but only for a second. Then, like always after I explode, the heat drained from my face down my throat again and I felt sick.

I turned back to where Jersey Plates stood waiting in the shade. She wasn't there. Her car was gone, the little red Civic. Except for me, Plato, and my berries, the lot was empty. I walked in her direction anyway, thinking up all kinds of explanations, excuses, and apologies. She had dropped the driftwood in the dirt, and when I picked it up it was still warm from her hand.

I hoped she would come back the following day—she said her vacation was for a week—but she didn't come back. It was a good afternoon otherwise, with a record amount of sales. Nice people, too. They couldn't believe how blue the berries were— how cool, firm, and delicious. I told them about the antioxidants that make them the world's healthiest food, then explained how it was a fruit with a tremendous amount of character and dignity. Bluets, the French explorers called them, when they first came upon this coast. In August the hills were powdered blue with them and the sailors crowded the rails to stare in wonder.

I thought about her for the rest of the summer—I'm thinking about her now, sipping coffee at Annie's, watching the ice floes bob up and down on the tide, killing off another winter. Jersey Plates. She joins the long list of women I only knew for a few minutes who meant more to me than any girlfriends or wives.

Once in Boston at an Aerosmith concert I hit it off with a girl sitting across from me, a dancer with curly red hair and breasts so perfect they made me want to cry in happiness, but somehow we got separated when the concert ended, and though I tore through the crowd after her and shouted her name we couldn't find each other and she was lost.

Another time I picked up a woman hitchhiking on Route 1, a teacher from Slovenia, and we laughed and laughed all the way to Camden, but somehow the timing wasn't right to make it anything better. And once on a beach I talked to a young mother lying on the next blanket, and we had everything in common in the world, but she was a young mother with two cute kids, and it could go no further than those perfect few minutes, with the tide edging ever closer to our toes.

There's more I could mention, but you get the point. It's the trick life likes to play on me, holding out love, snatching it back again. The good thing is I've gotten used to it over the years. The sad thing is I've even come to like it.

# A FRIEND OF
# MILLYARD MUSEUM

AT THE END OF THE BUS RIDE always waited an old man.

At the aquarium he slapped his hands together dressed like a seal. At the farm he met them with a baby lamb in his arms. At the art museum he wore a beret and a paint-stained sweatshirt. It seemed the same man they shuffled around just to greet them, dressing him differently each time, but Abroon understood there must be many old men in this country who had nothing better to do than meet school buses, hand out the tickets, tell children what they were facing.

So it puzzled him, there not being an old man this time. Ms. Rogers got off the bus gingerly, put her phone to her ear, then, when no one came out to welcome them, made a little speech on her own.

"Listen up, fifth-graders! You are to proceed without running to the entrance and wait in the lobby until everyone is accounted for. There will be a meeting room to the right where we will leave our backpacks and snacks. Millyard

Museum is grouped into five different galleries or themes and you are to choose one to write your report on once we get back to class."

She paused and looked meaningfully down at them, especially at Ganim and Ivanko smirking off to the side, their hands already balled into fists.

"We will show the museum staff the highest respect possible, is that understood? We will not disrespect them in any way, nor will we disrespect ourselves or the reputation of Horace P. Conte Public School."

Abroon, last off the bus, was convinced the driver had mistakenly dropped them off in a canyon. Brick walls rose sheer from either side of the pavement, and even by craning his head back he couldn't make out the tops. It was very old brick—the mortar was pitted and gray. "Prison," the other students immediately decided. But why would they go on a school trip to prison?

Ms. Rogers went inside to find the old man, leaving the parent volunteers to watch over them. It had started snowing the moment they left school, and already there was enough for Ganim and Ivanko to make iceballs. It was the second time Abroon had ever seen snow. The first had been on Tuesday, walking with his mother back from afterschool program to their room.

"Ah, come at last!" she mumbled, not happily.

She tried warning him about things ever since they came, but always ended up muttering, stumbling, hesitating, not sure where, in this new country, the dangers really lurked. In talking to women who had lived here longer she had finally settled on a definite enemy: snow. It snowed when December came, they would have to steel themselves to that fact. Even people who had lived here all their lives often went crazy under it, it fell so hard and lasted so long.

*Mother, why are you so afraid of snow?* he wanted to ask. *Dressed in robes, there is no place it can touch you.* But she knew, she insisted, she warned, shaking him hard to the lesson would sink in. Snow was the great danger here, and with his father away looking for work again they would have to face it on their own.

Here in the mill yard it didn't drop from the sky like it had the first time, but floated upwards in the wind, flakes that were hard and red and heavy. Was that what they had built here in the old days? Bricks made of snow? If they could rise like this then they could fall, and if they could fall they could hurt, so maybe his mother was right after all.

The students filed through the entrance, stomped their feet on the black wooden floor, then, when Ms. Rogers quickly shushed them, deposited their coats and backpacks where they were told, fished their note pads out, formed in line again, waited. An old man was bound to appear now, with a button on his chest or his ID hanging from a shoelace. Instead, a pretty woman even younger than Ms. Rogers came over and started in with a talk she had obviously given many times before.

"Welcome to Millyard Museum, boys and girls. Today, you will learn what life was like in a textile mill of a century ago, when even young children worked long hours at the looms to support their families, many of them new Americans, through difficult times. We will begin in Gallery Number One, showing the many cultures that have dwelled here at the river's great falling place even in the days before Western Man came to these shores."

"Cell phones off!" whispered Ms. Rogers. But very few of them had phones.

The walls were brick like on the outside, but a richer, deeper red, as if they were heated, not chilled. They tapered inwards to a gift shop and cash register, which is what everything in this country did—narrow down to a choke point, a barrier, a cash register—and walking through it without paying surprised Abroon, even after all the school trips he had been on.

He kept himself to the back of the group, not just from shyness but because he preferred having life out in front of him where its surprises could be avoided, though this didn't always work. There was a water fountain by the restrooms and he made the mistake of bending over for a drink. Instantly, from out of the shadows on either side, hands jumped out and hammered his head down on the metal spigot hard enough to draw blood.

Ganim. Ivanko. They hardly bothered laughing—victims like him weren't worthy of laughter—and when they saw his lip all it drew from them were business-like nods. What hurt most was that Jabes was with them, the Dominican who had just started school, the one who up until that moment he thought might be a friend.

"Abroon! Stop dallying, you need to keep up!"

He remained where he was in the darkness, dabbing at his lip with his sleeve. He was alone and then he wasn't alone. The old man, the old man he'd been expecting, stood watching him from the edge of the gift shop, having witnessed the whole episode. He wasn't dressed in costume like the seal man, but in gray pants held up by suspenders and a tired-looking suit coat that sagged down off his shoulders.

He had a badge, or at least a button, but it wasn't very official looking, and Abroon's first thought was that he was an impostor.

And he was older than the other old men. His face looked like it was chipped out of old brick, outside brick, the brick that generated snow. He wobbled just standing still, looked like he was going to fall, but then he plunged his hand into his pants pocket, came out with a pistol-like metal tube, stuck it down his throat, inhaled. It steadied him enough he could meet Abroon's stare, give him just as much concentration as he was receiving. It wasn't an angry look and it wasn't a pitying look and it wasn't the look of someone who particularly cared that a fifth-grader had just been bullied.

*Get over it*, the look seemed to say. *Go join the others. Take what comes.*

"Abroon!"

He rinsed his lip in the fountain, touched it to make sure he'd gotten the blood, then put himself at the back of the group where it had stopped in the first wide gallery. It showed what the inside of the mill had looked like in 1910, with paintings on the wall and diagrams of the machinery and glass display cases behind which were examples of the cloth they had made, examples of the threads. There was a dummy made up to look like an old-fashioned rich lady, dressed in the same kind of cloth on display. Beside her, as always, Shazfa wrote furiously on her pad.

The guide pointed to a dark opening in the wall that looked like an oven witches would use.

"This was the penstock where water from the river was diverted inside to turn the axle that powered the looms. During times of high water the mill would operate around the clock. It was not uncommon for shifts at the looms to last from 5:00 in the morning to 9:00 at night, with a lunch break of twenty minutes and five minutes to go potty. The ones working the looms were often fourteen and fifteen-year-olds, young immigrant boys and girls not much older than you, and they never made more than thirty cents a day."

Ms. Rogers vigorously nodded.

"Not much older than *you*."

"And over here we have a hands-on exhibit I think you'll find challenging. The thread was fed onto the loom using something called a shuttle. It was oval-shaped and very heavy, and yet the boys and girls would have to keep it moving to the loom's rapid back-and-forths. The shuttles were often crafted of flowering dogwood because the wood is very hard and can be polished into a smooth finish that didn't cause splinters. Very often the looms would go so fast the workers fell behind and the shuttle would fly off and strike them. A fifteen-year old girl who worked here invented a way to prevent this. Mattie Knight was her name and it made her one million dollars."

Was that who the rich lady dummy was supposed to be? Mattie Knight with breasts square as shoeboxes? Abroon saw Shazfa look up at her with new respect.

The other students lined up to try operating the model shuttle and loom—the shuttle had blue thread wrapped around it like a stick holding kite string. There was a big orange button and when you pushed it the loom started going back and forth just like it did in 1910, and you had to put your hands on the shuttle and push it forward at the same rate of speed. No one managed to do this, not even Ganim, Ivanko, or Jabes. They shoved aside the others, swaggered up to the shuttle, put their meaty hands on it, started pushing, but the loom was always faster—three times faster, four times faster, blindingly faster—and they ended up slapping the case in frustration and turning away like they didn't care.

The guide lady waved them into the next gallery—Ms. Rogers waited to make sure there were no stragglers. Abroon fell into line, got patted on the head, then, where the hallway darkened again, doubled back so he had the shuttle machine all to himself.

It was the height of a piano, which meant he had to raise himself up on tiptoes. The loom itself was under a glass dome, but the shuttle extended out on matching wooden rails and its bar is what you had to keep pace with once you pushed the button to make it start.

He pushed it—afraid to, afraid not to. With a soft cricket chirping the loom started moving toward his side of the glass, and he slammed his fists on the shuttle to send it forward to meet it. It did—he felt a moment of great satisfaction—but the loom was just warming up. He spread his hands apart, crouched, readied himself, tried bringing his eyes down to his fingertips—and yet he was far too slow, and the loom's hum became more like a mocking laugh. None of the other students had moved the shuttle as fast as he had, and yet it wasn't anywhere near fast enough.

"Lock your wrists. Use the heel of your hands and just kiss it, don't shove. You're chasing—let the loom come to you. Concentrate. Can you concentrate?"

The old man stood behind him with an expression that could have been of great scorn or great sadness—Abroon was good at reading looks, but this one he'd never seen.

Up close, he looked not just old but completely broken, as if a knife had sawed away at his middle, so his back peeled one way, his belly and legs peeled the other. Only his pants held him up, his suspenders. He hadn't shaved in days, and the stubble wasn't white and dignified like with elders he remembered from their village, but gray and dirty, a beard fit for goats.

"Here, try again."

The old man reached forward to push the button. Challenged, Abroon did better—he met the loom three times in succession. The faster it went, the dizzier he felt, so it wasn't just his hands that felt slow, it was whatever lay at the center of him, made up his balance. He thought about closing his eyes and doing it all through touch so the loom's blur wouldn't interfere, but he was afraid the old man would mock him.

"Hard? You expecting easy? Imagine what it was really like. Imagine the noise—the mill girls screamed just to be heard by the girl next to them. And the dirt. There were particles of cotton in the air finer than dust and half the workers had tuberculosis. The owners kept the windows closed even in summer. Picture the foreman coming around to make sure you were working fast enough—nothing was ever permitted to slow the looms down. A rap on the head? A kick on the ass? That was the least of it. Show any gumption and you were out, without another mill in the state willing to hire you . . . Stopping? Giving up? Arms hurt already? Then picture doing this fourteen hours straight."

His arms did hurt—looking down, he saw a stringy rippling motion in his forearms that was totally independent of him. He rubbed them furiously, unwilling to let the old man see and yet needing to stop it instantly before the rippling spread.

"Somali are you?"

It wasn't a question and Abroon didn't answer. He pressed the button again, this time angrily, stepped away from the shuttle . . . *There, do it yourself old man!* he said under his breath . . . then ran to the next gallery to catch up with the others.

The boys had gathered around an old fire engine pulled by big plastic horses—it looked like brassy pots and pans stacked upside down on a carriage. The girls stood with their pads under a sign reading *Tenement Life*, with zinc washboards and paintings of angels and beds made out of iron, all crammed into a space the size of a closet. A display to the side was labeled *Ticking*, and showed examples of coarse-looking fabric with fine lines down the middle. *Ticking*. He liked the sound of it, and for the first time wrote on his pad.

What interested Abroon most were the pictures of what the mill had looked like a hundred years ago. Pictures of wagons being unloaded of big cotton bales, pictures of the river in flood, pictures of girls in smocks and aprons standing by looms like the one operated by the button, only a hundred times larger. Pictures of workers posed outside in the millyard, hundreds of workers, more people than he had ever seen inside one photo, all from that distance looking very pale, very serious.

None of their other trips had interested him like this. He would have liked time to study every photo, read every caption, start boring in on the lessons they were surely meant to teach.

But there were snacks now—Ms. Rogers was very serious about snacks—then a short film in the auditorium, then to his great disappointment they were lining up for the bus. The snow was heavier than before, and yet the bricks still tossed it skyward with their peculiar trick. He hadn't realized before how beautiful walls could be, rising so straight, so solidly, as if whoever built them intended them to last a thousand years. None of the buildings he knew had that kind of dignity. The school was new but already the ceilings sagged. The shops his mother took him to were all made of cement. The room they lived in was smaller than the tenement, their sheets and towels coarser than any ticking.

The mill's walls were so high they stayed in sight after the bus pulled away—he twisted in his seat to see. Even after they crossed the highway, even through the snow, he could still make out the reddish crenelations that ran along the top. It was a discovery and a major one—that the mill could be seen from his school, had been visible all along if only he'd known.

Their trip to the mill was on Wednesday. On Thursday before after-school program he went to the principal's office and called his mother. He was going to Shazfa's house to work on homework, he said. His mother would have to call the principal right back and give permission.

He had lied to his mother before, but not over anything this big, and he blamed her for making him do it. Her warnings about snow—he was tired of hearing them. It was snowing again today, but who cared? He pulled the cuffs of his pants down as far as he could, hoping they would cover his sneakers. His jacket had a hood that was too small, but by bunching it up he made a collar that kept his neck dry.

He waited out by the playground until the buses left,

then started running toward the river, taking the streets that made it easier to see the mill's walls and avoiding those that hid them. He got beeped at by cars, almost fell into a lake of slush, changed directions to avoid some boys who looked even thicker and meaner than Ganim and Ivanko, but ended up exactly where he intended in less time than he thought.

That left one hurdle—the choke-point, the entrance, the cash register. The old man sat beside it on a stool, and if he looked old yesterday it was nothing compared to how old he looked today. *He's going to die and I'm going to get blamed for it*, Abroon decided. Again and again he sucked on the metal tube, as if it were a life-saving kind of cigar. There seemed to be a cloud of mist over his head, snorted up by his nose. His shoulders were so loose and lifeless they sagged down to his hips like the smocks the mill girls wore in all the photos.

So he was slow in spotting him—and, when he did, slow in changing expressions.

"Yeah?" he said, without much interest.

Abroon could run—an old man like that would never catch him—but then his arm came up in a gesture that was a shrug and yet not a shrug.

"Why the hell not."

Did that mean he could go in? He hurried past the penstock to the shuttle machine and loom. The museum was empty this time of day so he didn't have to wait on line. He leaned in toward the glass dome, rubbed it with his sleeve to make sure he could see clearly, readied himself by the shuttle, tried remembering the old man's suggestions. Heel of hands. Hit with the heel of hands. Concentrate on the shuttle, not the loom, so things don't blur.

He took the deepest breath he was capable of, bent his fingers back so they were out of the way, hit the button. The exhibit hadn't been used for a while, so it was slow to get going, giving him the illusion he could keep up. Yesterday it was three back-and-forths before he fell behind. Today he got six, even seven, before the loom raced ahead of him and the mocking noise came back.

He concentrated, tried again. Eight back-and-forths. He tried again. Ten back-and-forths. He tried again. Four back-and-forths. He tried again. Three. The loom was playing with him, stoking his confidence then crushing it.

During one of these attempts the old man took up a position behind him where he could watch on his stool with a cup of coffee—he kept mumbling words of advice that sounded like scolds. *Make yourself into a machine. Steel yourself. Think of what they faced. Little girls could do this why not you?*

Abroon, concentrating, said nothing back. He was uncomfortable with people who didn't know about his silences, which took time to understand. Took questions not answered. Pauses not picked up on. Stares he blinked away from. Stories told him with none he told back.

But the old man didn't seem to expect him to talk, as long as he listened—their bargain was clearer for not having been spelled out. He had let him in past the cash register, but like everything in this country it wasn't for free.

"Goldilocks and King Kong. Bosnians, right? The ones who hurt you?"

He pointed toward the water fountain.

"And their little lapdog? Columbian? Dominican? You'll need to watch out for that one—I saw how he joined in. And that smart girl, the one who ran on ahead. Pakistani, right? You need to pay attention to all this. Sunni? Shiite? Bhutanese? Nepalese? A lot rides on knowing the differences ... Here, give your hands a rest, follow me."

There was a gallery past the one with the fire engine—a smaller room with a vaulted ceiling and more photos than anywhere else.

"Offices were here, the bookkeepers—they wanted something that looked like a church ... Okay, stop right here. This picture down low? All the mechanics, the master ones who kept the looms operating. Taken in spring 1916 when the war was on and the mill made uniforms for the Brits and Krauts both. See him? Sixth one in from the right middle row."

Abroon bent over to count. The sixth man in was taller than the others, more serious looking, with a face like the bark on a log.

"My father, Kaarle Laukkannen. It means strong in Finnish. My father was a Finn."

This last word meant nothing to Abroon, but he stared anyway, glad to have at least one of the faces named and identified.

"You know about Finns? Of course you don't. Born agitators. Anarchists. The Wobblies had lots of them. They made the best union organizers and they made the best mechanics. You wanted your looms to operate smoothly, you went out and hired yourself a Finn . . . Other than that? Plenty of Irish, of course. Italians, though not as many as other mills. Yankee farm girls, but they were here to marry the bosses and once they did they never looked back. But there were seventeen thousand workers here by 1925. Seventeen thousand! And you know who most of them were? French.

Frenchies. French-Canadians down from Quebec where they were starving on their farms. P.Q.s they called them or sometimes Canucks."

He tugged Abroon to the next gallery in. There were more pictures here, but now they were all of churches and christenings and picnics and parades.

"Little France, they called it, where the Canucks lived around their cathedral. They had great dances, but outsiders like my father got beat up if they flirted with the girls. Beautiful girls. Everyone knew the French girls were prettiest. But that's not the point here. The point is that the French always did what their betters told them, they never thought for themselves. All those centuries thinking that priests must always be right switched over to thinking the bosses must always be right. That's why the owners hired them—they did what they were told, asked no questions, never organized. My father recognized that right away, that the French were his enemies. He had good things to say about all of them, from Poles to Croatians, but Frenchies he despised."

A bell sounded behind them—a woman's voice came through a speaker announcing the museum was closing in fifteen minutes. Abroon hoped the old man would ignore it, but he turned nervous and fussy, putting his hand on Abroon's back and hurrying him out past the fire engine and the penstock and the cash register to the entrance.

"Here," he said, reaching under the counter for a button. "Wear this when you come back and no one will say boo."

*A Friend of Millyard Museum* the button read. It showed the mill with a sun rising over the walls. Abroon, bending his head down, pinned it to his shirt.

He couldn't come back the next day, nor the day after

that—use the Shazfa excuse too often and his mother was bound to find out. Instead, he pried a dowel off a broken chair in their room, brought string from art class, made a shuttle he could practice with before going to sleep. He didn't tell anyone about this. The button he wore on the inside of his shirt so no one could take it.

There was a snow day the following week, with no school. His mother didn't know about snow days—she walked him to the bus stop just as always—and so he was able to go to the museum without having to lie.

The old man wasn't on his stool, but he had left his smell behind, a mix of liniment and pee. Abroon went right to the shuttle machine, pushed the button, bore his hips in close to the display case, started in with his hands. Right away he saw a difference. The week of practice had sharpened his reflexes so even on the first try he met the loom twenty times in a row. The computer games the other students played always went to a new level if you got too good at them, and the loom seemed to know the same trick—the faster he went the faster it went. Still, he managed twenty-five times in a row, thirty times, and was just on the point of throwing his arms up in victory when everything blurred up again, the loom blinded him with its instantaneous back-and-forths, his wrists and forearms spasmed, and, as always, he fell hopelessly behind.

"Better. Much better. You're starting to understand. But you're still not harnessing the right part of you. Hands, fingers, and wrists are important, but you need more than that, things that lie a lot deeper than muscle. And that surprises me, a smart kid like you. Why in hell can't you figure out what it takes?"

Abroon reached for the button but the old man's hand blocked it off.

"Follow me."

They walked through the big gallery to the small chapel-like one, stopped at another wall of pictures and paintings. Inside a big frame was an old newspaper with a black headline: *STRIKE!* The old man pushed him toward it, but Abroon, instead of reading for himself, waited for the story that was bound to come.

"It's 1928, right? The mill is humming along, making record profits, and they haven't had the kind of trouble they had down in Lowell or Lawrence because everyone knows French-Canadians don't strike. The owners cut back on wages and increase the speed of the looms, and no one says boo. No one except my father and his allies among the mechanics. Working quietly, then out in the open, they get half the workers to agree to walk out. Strike! The first time ever. For a day everyone is ecstatic—they're finally fighting for their rights, their dignity. But then the owners bring the national guard in and scabs and the next day it's over and everyone has gone back to the looms like it never happened."

Abroon couldn't make sense of this, the strike word meant nothing, but he understood the old man's tone. Bitter, angry bitter—bitter like the iceballs boys would throw at him at recess. Down the wall from the newspaper was another big picture, this one showing a hundred workers posed in the mill yard at a retirement party or company celebration.

"Wasn't good enough for the owners, just breaking the strike. They had a score to settle. I want you to look closely at three men, memorize their features. First row left. Second row fourth in. Third row center. See them? Ordinary guys, right? Bland looking, smiling, harmless."

He pressed his thumb on their faces, one, two, three.

"This fat one is Adolphe Trottier and the one with the hat is Pascal Robichaud and this bald one is Louis Bergeron. They came up to my father just before closing time when he was adjusting the tension on a willow machine in Building Three, with revolving spikes for cleaning raw fiber—came up to him, took his hands, held them down on the plate as the spikes rammed down . . . The owners felt bad about this. Full of remorse. Offered my father a job as night watchman at half the salary he made as a mechanic, and he had to swallow his pride and take it, because he had me to raise now and my sister . . . Joke was on them in the end, those Frenchies. Mill closed in 1929 because the owners didn't want to deal with any more of that strike nonsense. Moved the whole shooting match to Georgia, put ten thousand men and women out of work, left only these buildings, never once looked back."

Like an iceball to the head—that's what Abroon thought about as the old man explained. The angry surprise of it on the forehead, then the sting, then the bitter melting down the throat.

"Ancient history, right? All in the past? You ever hear of offshoring? Downsizing? Robots? There are lots of ways now to crush a man's hands. You think I work here just as a hobby?"

The old man must have worried his anger had gone too far. He walked Abroon back through the galleries to the one that showed the kinds of ticking they had made there, all the beautiful different fabrics. But his heart wasn't in it, explaining about these other exhibits. The phone rang by the cash register and he limped off to answer it, leaving Abroon near the shuttle machine. He pressed the orange button, but when the loom started flying he just stood there and watched.

He had intended to spend the entire snow day in the museum, but he worried now that his mother would have learned about it and called the school. The old man had sunk back onto his stool and had to put his hands under his chin in order to look up.

"You have someone waiting for you? Someone watching out for you? Here, stick out your hand. My name is Carl Lauk, like my father only American."

"Abroon."

"Abroon?" The old man closed his eyes, finally nodded. "Okay, got it. Abroon. A strong name, stronger than mine. Be careful out there, Abroon. Watch your back with those Bosnians."

The following week was school vacation and he spent it at a program offered by the shelter for anyone who had ever lived there, not just now. The children all coughed—he came down with a virus that kept him from going to the mill for another month. By the time he used the Shazfa excuse again the sunshine had started melting the snow, and when he got to the museum there were sparrows pecking at the mortar on the walls, red-headed sparrows, acting like they were working to take the mill apart.

He didn't go in right away—he reached under his shirt for his Friends button, put it on the outside where it belonged—and when he did there was an old man on the stool, but a different one from last time. This one seemed zipped up tighter, straighter, and his smile made the corners of his mouth curl, so it was like a smiley face his bright shirt turned yellow.

A smiley face—and yet his voice sounded solemn and regretful.

"You the Somali boy?"

Abroon nodded.

"Your friend . . . Sad, very sad . . . A long battle . . . Very brave . . . Really knew his history . . . Sometimes these things—"

That's as far as he went with his explanation. His mouth corners curled up again, and he pointed to Abroon's button.

"You're good to go, son."

There was a big new banner that hadn't been there last time—*Woven in Time; 11,000 years at Amoskeag Falls*— but Abroon ducked under it and ran straight to the loom machine.

He pushed the button, but didn't touch the shuttle even when the loom began flying. The old man's face and looks he had already forgotten, but he remembered his words, how he told him he must use another part of himself if he ever wanted to master it, a secret spot that would make his hands move faster. But why had he made it into a riddle? Why hadn't he just told him? That's what people did in this country, hide truth under questions they knew the answers to and wouldn't tell. They asked questions at school, questions at the state offices, questions at clinics and shelters, always another question, and they either looked bored waiting for your answer or eager that you would answer wrong.

It made him angry, thinking of this—angry enough he shoved his belly up against the display case, brought his hands down to the shuttle, shoved it in fury toward the advancing loom.

His anger led to deeper angers, so he thought of the bullying in school, how his mother's courage was wasting away little fear by little fear, the lie that his father was gone looking for work. He thought of the clothes that were always too tight on him and smelled of whoever had owned them before. He thought of Ghalyia and Tamir mocking him for not having a phone. He thought of free church dinners where his mother wouldn't let him eat all he wanted because it wasn't polite—thought of American words in big letters that burned you like brands, TANF and IEP and EBT. He thought of the pitying looks his teachers would give him, followed immediately by looks of exasperation. He thought of how bitter this latest trick was, old men disappearing before you could prove to them what you could do.

He thought of all these things, the anger went from his heart to his arms to his wrists to the heels of his hands, stiffened them, quickened them, made them into springs, so each time the loom swung toward him he was ready to send it back. His muscles understood, his seeing, so the time when he was hopelessly slow already seemed the distant past.

The loom was fast, but he was faster. A hundred back-and-forths. A thousand back-and-forths. All day if that's what it took. Fourteen hours in a row. Day after day. Year after year. Back and forth, back and forth. Forever.

# STARS FELL ON ALABAMA

CALL IT SHYNESS, but for years it seemed a more powerful force than that, a wind that did with me what it wanted. At church with my family it blew me to the last pew in back, but even that wasn't far enough, I could still feel everyone's eyes staring at me out the back of their heads, so I would hide on my knees and pretend to pray. Playing baseball it whirled me to the distant outfield, then, after my fourth error in one inning, away from the game altogether. In school it squeezed me to the edge of the cafeteria where the sullen, silent kids pretended to be friends. The only time I felt free of its pressure was alone in my room with my books, where at last I had a rail to grab, a place I could stand my ground.

My family didn't call it shyness, but only *that*. "We need to get that looked at," my father said when I ran from the outfield and hid in the woods. "That doesn't seem to be so bad today," my mother said, days when I actually managed to appear in public. "That's pathetic," my sister Cherry said, when I hid in the basement from her friends.

Cherry was right. Pathetic, to think that even the thought of attending the town's Fourth of July celebration on the lake made me panic. This wasn't just any Fourth of July celebration, but the 200th anniversary of the town's founding. Money had been raised for fireworks, the first time this had ever been done, and all winter long when I went to the village store I dropped dimes in a big glass jar.

Still, *that was that*. All those people would be there, all those girls. I felt nervous in the morning, scared in the afternoon, terrified by evening. My mother carried our picnic basket out to the truck, my father hammered impatiently on the horn, but I still lay on my bed with a book over my face, the words pulled down into my eyes.

I don't know how I finally found the courage. "That's ridiculous," Cherry said, when she saw my expression. But she was a good big sister, and she yanked me up on the truck's bed just as my father stepped on the gas.

Our lake was beautifully set in a bowl of hills, but the town beach was borderline shabby. A grassy meadow to park on, a narrow strip of trucked-in sand, and then, dominating it all, a wooden lifeguard stand so tall and imposing it was known as the Washington Monument. The far side of the lake was where the rich summer people lived. Already, the moment I hopped down from the truck, I could see Roman candles shooting up from their docks.

"Let's find a space," my father said, grabbing the picnic basket and flashlights. "Donnie? You run ahead and scope things out."

My mother was on the Fourth of July committee, and she and her friends had hung Christmas lights over anything that would support them and draped bunting over everything else. It was crowded already, people streaming in from the nearby towns. Vendors sold light sticks and necklaces. A clown juggled pie plates. The town band did its best on Sousa. Firemen served chicken under their tent. Discarded watermelon slices lay on the grass like discarded smiles, and I remember being pleased with myself for seeing them like that—as discarded green and red smiles.

Everyone smoked in those days—the fumes added an explosive, gunpowdery feel to the celebration. And beer. There was plenty of beer. The smell formed a second, higher lake that fizzled up my nose and made me dizzy.

"How's about right here?" my father said, pointing to a patch of grass near the ice cream stand. He extended his arm, squinted down it toward where the fireworks crew rammed tubes into the mud by the boat launch. "Perfect sight line, just perfect."

"Will they fall on us?" my mother wanted to know.

Assured they wouldn't, she spread the blanket out, my father anchored the sides with soda cans, then with a regretful, apologetic look in my direction, they all immediately disappeared. They had too many friends to stay with me dealing with *that*. My father was town clerk, my mother had all her committees, and Cherry was the most popular girl in high school. I could trace their progression through the crowd by the happy, laughing rings that formed in their wakes.

I wasn't about to sit alone in total conspicuousness. I started for the barbecue tent, since it was darker there, more secret, but some girls my age were helping with the clean-up, and that shunted me back out toward the sand. Tough older kids stood slouched in a circle punching each other's stomachs, and that acted like another bumper, deflecting me to their right toward the water's edge. "Hello Donnie," a girlish voice purred, but after one delicious, impossible moment I realized it was another Donnie, not me.

I came to the Washington Monument. Girls had climbed to the top, and their legs dangled down like peach-colored tendrils from a wooden vase. I could have reached and stroked them, they hung so close, but now, as if sensing my presence, they drew back in alarm. A rocket had exploded high over the lake. It was a test fire—the fireworks crew wanted to see if it was dark enough to begin. The town band, misreading its cue, launched into the Star Spangled Banner, and those on the blankets now struggled to their feet.

I pressed my hand over my heart like everyone else, and for a moment this helped to calm it down. Over to my right, wearing a baggy Hawaiian shirt, stood Mr. Steffen, the only teacher in school I could actually talk to. He waved to me, pointed toward the sky, arced his hand to pantomime a leaping fish.

"Think the bass will get scared?"

I would have liked to go up to him, talk fishing the way we often did, but his wife was there, and she was so redheaded and pretty I couldn't look at her without blushing.

*Thwack.* Like a pinball off a flipper I rolled helplessly on.

The geography of this needs explaining. The old people sat on lawn chairs back by the parking field. The inner ring was families, most of them lying on blankets. The teenagers stood in packs near the beach. My shyness had detoured me around them into the water, so my sneakers and socks were now soaking wet. The bottom dropped off sharply there, enough so I felt gravity tugging me out. To get back to my family I would have to resist this, wade back in, run the gauntlet of everyone's stares.

For one indecisive moment I teetered there in the dark, knowing I must go back in, knowing that was impossible. From the circle nearest me, in the hush that came before the first explosions, I heard very distinctly the phrase "Two-ton balloon." It was soft, it came coated in giggles, and I naturally assumed it was meant for me.

I was husky, not fat—my mother was very careful to make the distinction. And yet it was just the sort of taunt I had been expecting all night, it's why I kept turning away from anyone who knew me, until here I was, waist-deep in the ink-colored lake. People saw me now, or at least my silhouette, and one man gestured angrily for me to come back in. Swimming during fireworks was prohibited, and for a moment I thought he was wading out to get me.

I was too embarrassed to go back in—my clothes were wet, maybe even transparent. My only option was to pretend I was in the water deliberately, that I didn't give a damn for rules, being a wild and crazy teenager determined to take his swim. I waded out to where the sandy bottom turned rocky, stopped to pry off my sneakers, tugged my shirt over my shoulders, felt my glasses slip off, groped for them, had them in my hand, lost them again, then, well over my head now, suddenly myopic, started toward the middle of the lake slapping out the best Australian crawl my huskiness could manage.

The water felt warm and reasonably supportive, though it tasted salty, as if from too many soggy potato chips. The last landmark before the lake widened out was a wooden float people could dive from. I thought I would climb to the top, wait there in relative safety for the fireworks to finish, but when I got closer I saw a long, cruller-like shape stretched out across the middle, glistening in wetness. Some undulation in the lake's surface, perhaps even the wake created by my kicking, was enough to move the float slightly up and down. The shape divided itself into two, then, with a whispered murmuring sound, became one again, a tighter one, a one that gently hunched, rolled, and flattened.

I remembered a phrase from one of my books: "two lovers entwined." I had red that again and again, trying to understand what it must be like, to be one of two lovers entwined. Was that what I had stumbled upon? It was hard to tell without my glasses. I tried convincing myself that it was life jackets I was seeing, that it was two life jackets entwined, or maybe two snapping turtles. But even that tormented me, in the mood I was in. Who was I to laugh at turtles, me who wasn't entwined with anything?

I was past the float swimming into open water when the fireworks started, this time for real. Since I swam face down with my eyes open, the first one came to me as a white, strobe-like flashing across the bottom of the lake thirty feet below. One second I stared into the inky blackness, the next I saw boulders, weed beds and grottoes I never suspected were there. A charcoal-colored blob winged its way across this—a sting-ray, I thought in my stupor—and it was only with great effort that I realized it was my own downcast shadow.

That was explosion number one. Explosion number two came when I rolled over on my back. It was as if all the

Christmas lights had been torn from the trees on shore, whirled into a neon cloud, brightened a hundred times, blinding me past the power of blinking to ever make right. And the boom. Always before I enjoyed the boom, the percussive way it hit you in the chest, but now I took the force straight on my groin, and it seemed powerful enough to do me real damage.

Sparks shimmied down toward my face—without my glasses, they looked like molten drops of lead. They made a hot and angry sound, like they were being doused in water, and it took me several seconds to realized they were sizzling out in the air.

Two more went up, two more arced, burst, and fell. I decided that right there in the middle of the lake was the safest place to watch—*if* I could tread water long enough. By the time the fifth exploded, out of sheer desperation, I had reinvented the whole process; in swim lessons, they taught us to combine a scissors motion with a frog kick, stirring slowly with the arms. This didn't do it for me—frog kicks pulled me under. What worked better was waving my arms around like a little kid does when he's excited, flopping my wrists, meanwhile folding my ankles up to my butt like a Buddha repeatedly squatting down. "Understand the physics of water," our swim instructor told us, but here it seemed more about the water learning to understand the physics of me.

The rockets overhead like giant blossoms, burning snowflakes, waving flags—I saw what everyone else saw, at least at first. It took me a while to appreciate them differently. Mr. Steffen had taught us about the Big Bang in science, and that's what I began thinking about. One second the sky was black and infinitely empty, then next it was bursting apart in metallic light, scattering its energy with a huge flinging motion through the void. Then, just as quickly, with a regretful sighing noise, the energy and light were utterly extinguished. Birth, life, and death for the universe, a complete cycle every ten seconds right above my head.

The force of the explosions stirred me around in the water like I was an ice cube or leaf. One second I faced the *oohs* and *ahhs* coming from the town beach, the next I was looking toward the shore with the big summer homes. It wasn't totally black there, late as it was now. Their docks were decorated with lanterns that cast a creamy blue light, and above the saw-toothed trees that backed them hung the amber line left by the sunset.

The next firework was more a flare than an explosion—its hot solder color lingered in the sky for long seconds. By its light I could see a disturbance in the water in the direction of the summer homes, moving toward me from the open lake—a phosphorescent lift and fall, lift and fall. As it came closer, I understood it was from a swimmer's arms reaching and dipping, reaching and dipping, as he or she neared the magic circle in the center of which I spun.

It was a she. Her black bathing suit was darker than the water, and even if it wasn't, the next firework illumined a shape there was no mistaking. She must have seen me now, because she changed directions. Three more strokes, a final graceful yearning motion, and she was past the curtain where the sparks sizzled down, rolling over on her back, letting her body sink to the vertical until she was treading water only five feet away.

She seemed surprised to find anyone there, but not as surprised as you might think.

"You too?" she said. It was between explosions and she tilted her head to the side so she could make me out.

It could have meant nothing or it could have meant everything, and as usual I answered back with something dumb.

"You're safe here," I said. There was water in my mouth so I had to gulp. "The sparks won't ignite us or anything."

As graceful as she was at swimming, she had trouble treading water—I fought down the urge to offer her advice.

"They're all so impossible," she said, gulping like I had, only nicer. She brought her hand out of the water just far enough to point back to the far shore, the shore with the summer homes, the shore with the creamy light. "People!"

She was older than me, which was fortunate. If she were my age, I would have held my arms to my sides and deliberately sunk toward the bottom. And while I had no idea how women's ages worked, I would have guessed twenty-two or twenty-three. My myopia couldn't make our her features other than in a general, impressionistic way. Her shoulders were lithe and strong, so maybe she had been on the swim team in college. Her hair was short—the wetness pressed it tightly to her neck. She had nice ears. Her cheekbones were high, like an Iroquois princess's. I didn't think her face was particularly pretty, but beautiful, and that puzzled me, since I thought to be beautiful you had to be pretty first.

She must have put on suntan lotion earlier in the day—the scent still lingered. And she wore earrings, bright as diamonds. It made it seem she had plunged into the lake suddenly, in the midst of dressing for a party or something grand.

"The wedding and all," she said, as if reading my thoughts.

She arced her head, shrugged back her shoulders, floated face up with her arms outstretched. The water sculpted her there—we were way past mere physics—and she accepted the light on her face like it was a fine pinpoint spray of exactly the right temperature. It made it seem I was peeking at her in the shower—not all of her, just her head, neck, and hair.

Float there forever, I remember thinking. Float there forever so I can look.

She tilted her head to the side, launching her voice to me like a little boat. "I've never seen anyone tread water like that before."

Was she teasing me? Complimenting me? It didn't matter, she said it so gently. She waited until the light from the next firework lit things up, then patted the water like she was making room for me on a sheet.

"You'll enjoy them better if you float."

It's the good thing about being husky—floating is a snap. I rolled back my shoulders until I was reasonably horizontal, then let buoyancy lever up the rest of me. And she was right—it was much better that way. Treading water, craning back my head involved a certain amount of struggle, but lying flat I was able to surrender to the fireworks completely, let their beauty cast its spell.

It was past the halfway point now, and what was being launched was increasingly spectacular. Three would shoot up all at once, the purple arcing toward the east, the pink toward the west, but these were only decoys, teases, because the one you needed to watch for burst right in the center, a huge glassy fountain of red, white, and blue sparks. Before its light faded away they added in pinwheels, sizzlers, zigzaggers, corkscrews, and when they cooled out there were fireballs of yellow and carousels of emerald and gold.

My eyes blurred the colors as they dropped, and I strove mightily to find words that would do them justice. Pretty girl peach. Birthday candle pink. Aluminum foil silver. Sparks off a metal lathe. Flaming green licorice. The red of Cherry's nail polish.

One burst, the highest so far, reached its apogee overhead. I blinked as it flung out its light, then fixed my vision on one of the brightest sparks, followed it all the way down until it almost but not quite touched my chest. I felt pierced even so. Its color pierced me, then kept on going into the lake.

Neither of us said much, that was the best part. Back on the beach, people would be giving out those exaggerated *oohs* and *ahhs* or cheering or making smart remarks. It was much better to let the booms do the talking. I glanced over at her again, saw her staring straight up into the sky. Though I couldn't see them, I sensed that her eyes were closed—closed like someone memorizing something, closed like someone saying goodbye. It was a thought much older than I was myself, a great leap ahead in understanding, and yet I remember sensing that very strongly—that she was lying under the fireworks saying goodbye.

She must have sensed me watching, because she said something now, though it was more to the sky than to me.

"Stars fell on Alabama, huh?"

It was a funny thing to say—not funny funny, but funny wistful. Was that her name, Alabama? Was it a song title?

Was that where she was from? Here in Vermont the stars stayed obediently pinned to the heavens, they didn't fall— only maybe I was wrong on this, because here they were falling all around us, or as good as, their light raining down.

Even with the difference in our ages, I felt protective of her. I wanted to swat away any rogue sparks that threatened to burn her, but that wasn't enough for me, I needed a sterner test. I pictured something going wrong on shore, a misfire, a dud plunging down toward her like a guided missile, me folding myself over her middle to absorb the shock of it on my back. Save her, that's what I wanted to do. Dust sparks off her shoulders, smother flames on her bathing suit, wipe tears from her eyes.

"Hold onto your hat," I said. It was the best I could manage.

Above us, six fireworks spiraled skyward all at once, followed by a long empty pause when the sky stayed black. From shore, we could hear people groan. Everyone sensed that was the climax, the grand finale, and it was disappointingly abrupt. But I'd been to fireworks shows before, knew their trick, which was to create that false sense of anti-climax, then, after a long hesitation, burst out with the real finale.

That's what happened. The eruption of light and sound that now crested over us was triple anything that had come before. It was as if the fireworks crew had sneaked to the lake days before and planted tubes not just by the boat launch but in the wetlands and by the docks and in the woods—planted tubes and called in the air force, seeding the atmosphere with hot diamond brilliance. From all these secret orifices rockets spasmed their way skyward, rending the blackness, transforming it into shafts of unbearably bright color, so you couldn't stare directly at the intensity, and yet, from the suction of its energy, you couldn't bring yourself to look away. These fireworks didn't just explode and fade out, but hung for long seconds in the sky, especially the red ones, which seemed to have escaped the laws of gravity altogether.

In between booms I could hear girls screaming in shock and pleasure on the beach. The explosions and screams found the hills together, blended into one ecstatic cascade of sound, then, with startling contrast, ended in silence and the last trembling pendant-shaped sparks. And then when they too had vanished all that remained overhead were the stars that had been there all along, serene as they had ever been, unexplodable, indifferent.

Alabama—that's how I thought of her now—must have stopped watching before I did, because when I looked over to check if she was safe she was treading water much closer to me than before, within touching distance, so the water lapping her chest moved over and lapped mine. Our eyes met, or at least I think so—in the darkness, my myopia was total. I don't know if she laughed first or I laughed first, but in a moment we both laughed together. After the grand climax what else was there to do?

She twisted around so her mouth was very close to my ear and a little behind it. "How old are you?" she asked.

"Sixteen," I said, adding on a year.

She was all the way behind me now, past my neck around to my other ear. I could feel her inspecting me, appraising me, sizing me up.

"You look older than that. Younger than that. No, neither. You look just right."

She reached around and touched me then, though with the cushion of water I wasn't sure where. Above the waist, but was it on my heart, my nipple, my breastbone, my shoulder? I don't know where it was because I didn't feel it there, but through some magic transmission directly on my lips, which tingled and buzzed in a way that was new to me and indescribably electric. Even more mysterious was its taste—a peppermint coolness. How could touch carry taste?

I rubbed them, wanting to push the buzz in even deeper, or, failing that, to wipe it away so I wouldn't drown from sheer pleasure. I flopped my arm back to twist myself around, but she was already swimming away from me, with the same long, yearning strokes that had brought her to me in what already seemed the distant past.

This time there was no curtain of fire for her to cross. I saw the phosphorescent dipping of her arms, a shivery trail of bubbles, and then there was nothing but the lights on the shore she was heading for, and, much closer, the weak flashlights and damp sparklers shining from the shore that was mine.

In swimming back, my hands came down against soggy tubes of cardboard wadding that still smelled of gunpowder, so maybe we were in greater danger than I thought. The crowd that had pressed so close to the beach walked back toward their cars, blankets over arms, kids asleep on shoulders, lawn chairs clanking against lawn chairs, everyone guided by spotlights the firemen shone on the grass. A croaky male voice started singing Happy Birthday to the town, but people were too sleepy to join in.

My toes hit sand, then something plastic—my glasses, their frames bent but otherwise intact. I adjusted them on my nose, then emerged wet and dripping near the Washington Monument. I walked tall and straight, even though no one watched. Compared to my usual shuffle it felt like strutting.

The girls had all left. The families had left. I spotted Tom Bullthroat, our town miser, shining his lantern down looking for spilled pocket change. People on the fireworks committee were doing their best to clean up. Among them was Mr. Steffen, and he was the only one who saw me come out of the water.

He didn't seem surprised at this. He seemed to already know all about it, what had happened to me out in the lake. Someone who could explain the Big Bang theory had no trouble understanding bashful kids.

"So Donnie," he said gently. "Find any bass?"

I had no fast and funny answer for him. *No Mr. Steffen, something much better*, I could have said, but I still had years of work ahead of me before I found his kind of naturalness and ease. I probably mumbled something though. He made a go-scoot gesture with his garbage pail, and off I ran to find our truck.

That was forty years ago—and that's the hardest thing to get my mind around, that I can write the words *that was forty years ago*. There are still Fourth of July fireworks on the beach, though plastic tape goes up to prevent anyone swimming. I have no grandkids of my own, but my friends let me share theirs, make room for me on their blankets, pour me wine. Watching, I still sometimes wonder where near the heart Alabama touched me, now when all I mostly wonder about is where in this world of mystery the wondering part of me has gone.

# THE ZONE OF HABITABILITY

THAT'S THE WAY THE WORLD WORKS NOW I GUESS. A Jew born in Morocco becomes a Montana fishing guide. A Vietnamese woman I know finds work as a cowboy. One of my colleagues in the astronomy department was born in Cameroon to Bolivian parents. My fiancé grew up in New Zealand, majored in modern dance at Oklahoma State, and now runs a solar startup in Billings. People shuffle around geographies and destinies like never before.

"Yes, I understand all that," I told Rich when he surprised me with the trip. "Still, a Jew born in Casablanca is not someone you meet every day, particularly on a trout stream."

Rich, who was getting his backpack ready for his own weekend, smirked his cutest Dennis the Menace smirk.

"They claim he's the best fly fishing guide in Montana, only—"

"Only?"

"That's what they say about him. He's the best fishing guide in Montana, only—. You'll have to fill in the blank when you get home."

People were surprised, Rich and I racing off on separate trips a week before the wedding. But he likes rock climbing, I like trout fishing, and it seemed the perfect way to celebrate. We weren't spending money on bachelor parties or showers or anything traditional, and once we married, we told each other, we'd have 50 years to do things together.

I left the apartment at three in the morning, hit Livingston just as the sun was edging up over Emigrant Peak, grabbed some tea at a trucker's cafe, and was at the put-in by seven. A truck was already parked there, with an empty boat trailer on back, and the man who climbed down looked, from the groggy way he stumbled, as if he had slept there all night.

"Jonathan Chu," I said, sticking out my hand.

"Eli," he mumbled. "Eli, Eli, Eli."

Was he scolding himself? That's what I sounded like. The cold made the syllables snap like a whip.

"Nice to meet you, Eli. I'm really looking forward to fishing with you today."

"Are you?'

He stared at and around me now, not in a curious way, but like he was evaluating the larger world of which I was a minor, incidental part. He was a big man, with shoulders round from years of rowing driftboats, and I put his age at 49. He didn't wear guide clothes, not the nylon and fleece that's become their uniform, but faded gray work pants and matching shirt, making him look like he worked in a garage.

His face, what I could see of it in the mist, had large expressive features, though not the kind that had anything particularly cheerful to express. His nose was the saddest I ever saw on a man, though I can't tell you how I read that other than the way its weight dragged down his forehead, left it wrinkled. His complexion was pure leather, distressed leather, with dry white patches on his cheeks that looked like they needed to be oiled. Even so, he was tanner and craggier than any guide I'd ever encountered, as if he drew upon a weathering, a tempering, a lot more thorough than anything you could get just in Montana.

"So you want to fish, is that it?"

I held up my rod case. "Raring to go."

He shook his head, scowled with a fierceness that almost made me flinch.

"My boy busted parole last night. Busted it all to hell. And now?" He spat toward the river. "Goddamn caddis flies aren't hatching."

The second part seemed to sadden him more than the first. He waved his hand dismissively toward the bank, which seemed to mean I was supposed to climb in the driftboat.

"She's a beauty," I said, sliding myself down.

"Yaws."

"I sit up here?"

"Suit yourself. We're not going to catch shit."

He pulled on his waders—waders like my grandfather wore, of heavy brown rubber—then put his shoulder against the thwart and shoved us out. Immediately the current had us, taking us in hand with a vigorous side-to-side shake just to demonstrate who was in charge. The few guides I'd gone out with rowed like gondoliers, standing up at the oars, peering hopefully downstream, but Eli's posture was more like Charon on the river Styx, grim and huddled, his mouth just above the oars as if contemplating biting in.

"What fly should I tie on?" I asked, once I had my rod strung up.

"Know what piles are?"

"How about an Adams?"

"Know what they're like when they bleed?"

I tied on an Adams. At first I was blindly casting into fog, but when we rounded the first bend the sun exploded in a sudden burst that blew it all apart. Glorious! Mountains to the east, mountains to the west, the snow already sugaring up the summits, catching the sunlight and making it stick. The gullies, on the nearer ridges, shone cherry red, as if they'd just been polished and hadn't yet dried. Both banks, past their cottonwood crests, were mostly pastureland, and there was already enough of a breeze that the grass waved and tossed in its top-heavy autumn way.

"And what a great smell!" I said, breathing in. "Sage, right? And I think there's pine mixed in, too."

Eli, to humor me, sniffed.

"Oil shale," he said sourly. "We'll smell it all day. Pick your nose later and it'll be black."

"Isn't that hundreds of miles away?"

"Cast over there."

A back eddy dug into the right bank, nothing wider than a barrel, but I managed to put my fly right on its rim. A trout came up immediately, a big cutthroat hybrid, and I had it to the net before it realized it was even hooked.

*How's that?* I said, not out loud, but by glancing back at him. You're always trying to impress a guide when you first go out.

"Wife number three? Served me papers last week. Locked me out. *Shtupped* my best friend."

He seemed to be explaining this more to the trout than to me. And yet he was extraordinarily gentle with it, taking the hook from its lip like it was a baby with a boo-boo, then swimming it back and forth beside the boat waiting for it to regain its strength before letting go. Then and later, that's when he seemed most Semitic to me. He treated trout like they were his wealth, his livelihood, his camels.

"That's too bad," I said. "Your best pal? That's hard."

"VA screwed up my prescriptions. Hand me that rod."

Twice as fast as I could, his hands smoothly weaving, he tied on a dropper rig, worked out some line in two smooth shakes, then handed the rod back to me with one of his lesser frowns.

"Chinese shit. Watch it bust."

Was that meant to be personal? Nope—not even close. It had been clear from the first second that he could care less about me. I was just a guy he took fishing, like a thousand others, though maybe, just maybe, I cast better than most. But compared to the other possible attitudes he could adopt toward me, indifference was fine.

We had been paralleling a brush-covered island until now, and where it ended the water became faster and harder to read. Anyone who's fished from a driftboat knows they're remarkably stable when aligned with the current, but tippy when they go broadside. Playing the next fish, with both of us on the same side, there was only an inch or two of freeboard left before we swamped. Eli seemed used to this, but I decided to stay safely in my seat after that. Capsizing would do nothing for his mood.

And it was windy, now that the sun was high. It was behind us from the south and warming the air quickly.

"What a day!" I said again, just because I couldn't help it.

Eli squinted at the sky. "Rain later. Probably a twister."

The obvious trout water was along the banks where grasshoppers might plunk in, but he knew where the sunken ledges were in the middle and on either side of these lay fish. What's more, every new ledge required a different fly—he was always grabbing my line in mid-cast to tie on a new one—and, though at first I thought this was unnecessarily fussy, everything he tried seemed to result in an immediate hit. I'd decided on the drive down that a dozen fish would make for a good day, but I had those already—real cutts now, not hybrids, and that pinkish-red slash below their lips would flash through the water a breathless second before they hit.

"Kid sister's on food stamps and now they've cut them. So who pays for diapers? Eli pays for diapers, that's who pays for diapers."

I fought a small one, netted it myself.

"This whole side of the county, nothing but crystal meth. Like talking to zombies, cause that's what they are. Why'd we bother stealing it from the Blackfeet in the first place?"

Coffee from his thermos, a stop to pee, then a long stretch underneath some willows with four fish in a row. Me trying again.

"Aren't those caddis cases under the water there? Maybe we'll see a hatch after all?"

"That's where my mortgage is. Underwater."

Until now all my trout were on dries, but the next one took the nymph, and Eli had to spin the boat around a few times before I could get the right angle on it.

"Mining companies own this state. Governor's in their pocket. I had one of their bosses out here, liquored himself up and confessed. Montana mafia."

That was four—four sentences. Always before he stopped at three.

"Yes, I agree with you there, Eli. That's why I voted for the other guy."

I was staring down at the scum line toward a rise, but my back could feel his eyebrows arc.

"You voted? You fucking *voted*?"

He did something unexpected with that—he laughed. He laughed loud and he laughed long and it was the worst laugh I ever heard, with a deep grinding edge to it that pulverized any response you might come up with even before you came up with it, and ground it into hopeless naivety.

"He voted!" he said, this time toward the mountains. He did that more and more as the morning went on. Addressed his comments to the Absarokas, not me.

So I stopped trying to be sympathetic, tried blocking him out instead—and for a while it worked. The September sun was so warm I stripped down to my t-shirt and that made casting easier. With the preparations for the wedding, I hadn't fished more than two or three times all summer, and the muscle memory of casting, the elusive rhythm, was slow in coming back—but then it came back big-time, and all my happiness seemed centered in my shoulder, elbow, and wrist. I was clumsy at carpentry as a kid, terrible at sports, and a fly rod is the only tool I've ever learned to wield properly, fly casting the only athletic skill I've mastered. It's how I prove my manhood, though what I mean by that is difficult to explain.

But it paid off. I was reaching fish I knew most of his clients couldn't touch. One of them was nineteen inches long, deep bodied, vibrant with health and beauty.

Eli lifted it from the net, stared at it for far too long.

"You can see it in their eyes. Whirling disease. Chase their tails to get rid of the parasite and exhaustion finishes them off. He doesn't have it yet, but soon."

*Jesus Christ!* I felt like saying. Maybe I did say it, too, or at last whispered it under my breath. Bitching I could tolerate, a guy having a bad day, but what got to me was his tone, the way his deep voice turned everything into a pronouncement on mankind and nature and fate. And he made it seem wise, that was the worst part. Only a respected elder, someone who had meditated long and hard on life's condition, could make his voice that grim, that certain, and everything young in me wanted to throw it back in his face.

"That's a gorgeous spot up there," I said, making my voice go deliberately high and girly-girly just to vex him. "Good spot for lunch in that shade."

"Rattlers. They fuck there. Lunch spot's further down."

He pushed us toward shore, dropped the oars, unstrapped the cooler behind his seat, lobbed over a sack and some sodas.

There was a wide pool perfect for wading, and I took three good fish from the tail in between bites of lunch. Eli sat on a dead stump watching, making no secret of the flask resting on his knee. He held it up, but I shook my head.

"You make an awesome bologna sandwich," I said.

He couldn't be charmed, not that easily.

"Enough sodium to kill you."

"My dad used to make them, but not as good as yours."

"Never had a dad," he said, like it was a great stroke of luck.

"Good donuts, too."

"Killed my brother."

There was room on the stump, but I went over to the shade and stretched out where I wouldn't have to listen to him. The bank was so high and steep I could roll on my stomach and stare straight down into the water. It was different than anything we'd drifted over. The bottom was sand pebbled with flat blue rocks, and with the sun filtering through the effect was gentle, almost tropical, so for a moment I was tempted to strip naked for a swim. Trout, small ones, were tipping up to suck down midges whenever they crossed the sandy patches, but for once I had no desire to catch them, so beautiful and bird-like were their graceful levitations toward the top.

I'd heard that on a busy day in summer over a hundred driftboats would float this stretch of river, but we hadn't seen anyone else all day and it wasn't likely we would now. The only sign of man were contrails left by invisible jets, like ivory furrows tilled between clouds. So far from any cities I wondered where they were bound.

I knew what Eli would say, if I asked him. Bombers off to deliver their cargoes on people who probably deserved it. He had curled up for a nap, using a rock as his pillow. He talked in his sleep or bubbled or muttered—something made his lips move vigorously enough to tickle his nose and get him snorting. I listened, curious, but all I could make out was a raspy kind of V sound. *Vile*, I finally decided. In his sleep he was muttering the word *vile*.

•

He came awake, went over to squat on his haunches by the river, staring down toward its surface as if it were the only mirror he could trust. But no, it wasn't his face he was studying. He dipped his hands in, squinted at what they brought up, nodded, flung the water back through his fingers like blood from his wrists.

"Blue winged olives," he said. "Coated in pesticide. Trout spit them out."

He dug the anchor from the sand, shoved the boat back into the current, so for a moment I thought he was leaving without me. I climbed back into the bow, but not before blurting out something that was partly due to happiness, partly due to wanting to bust his chops. Don't like the way the world is heading, Eli? Well, try *this* on for size.

"I'm really fortunate to fit this trip in before the wedding. Richard is no fisher person. He wonders why anyone would deliberately torment a trout just for fun, and he doesn't actually approve of all this. But know what? It doesn't matter. We're soul mates. Except for astronomy, my life was zero before I met him. I love him very much."

There was no change in his expression, none that I could see. When your mouth is permanently fixed in a scowl, there's not much further it can drop. He reached into his fly box, squinted, tossed a fluffy one over.

"Tie this on," he grunted—his default answer for everything.

The wind swung around to the north in the afternoon and hardened. Navigating the boat became trickier, and I had to make sure I stayed centered so we wouldn't tip. I was still taking trout along the banks, but casting turned treacherous, and I worried I'd stick one in Eli's nose. He stood it for as long as he could, then grabbed my rod.

"Like this."

He threw a mend in the line while he cast, mid-air, a trick I can't do myself, and got the fly to land exactly where he wanted it despite the wind. It took a lot of skill, sensitivity, and timing, and yet, like with his rowing, he did it abruptly, almost brutally, as if it wasn't a skill he thought much of. And I wondered about that, even more than I wondered about his pessimism. How someone could be so good at something, something difficult, and not give the slightest damn.

The river widened the further downstream we floated, with spring creeks coming in from both east and west. With the increased flow, he had to devote more attention to rowing, and yet the challenge seemed to get him mumbling even faster than before. At first it was about his Iraq vet cousin who had just become homeless, then it switched to a pal who had joined a militia and ambushed a cop, and then he was complaining about the price of hookers in Bozeman bars.

He sat a foot behind me in the boat—at no point was his mouth further than twelve inches from my ear. By late afternoon, as fatigue kicked in, I began seeing things his way, despite all my efforts. An abandoned pioneer cabin on the bank didn't seem romantic and wistful like it would normally, but a symbol of defeat and decay. The cumulus, so blue on their undersides, now darkened into storm clouds and took on an ominous stacking. The trout, when I caught them, seemed emaciated, sick with whirling disease or about to be sick, and when I missed a good rise near a deadfall I was ready to cry.

But there was an odd thing to put against that. It was past five now, and most guides would have been thinking about what was waiting for them at home, but Eli seemed in no hurry—seemed, in fact, to be deliberately drawing out the day as long as possible. We'd drift past a good stretch of water, take a fish or two, then, instead of continuing with the float, he would turn around in his seat and row us upstream as fast as he could, so we could make another pass, then a third, then a fourth. He wanted more trout, that was the only explanation I could come up with. With 40 fish to the boat already, he still wanted more.

"People pretend to care, but they don't. Care about themselves. Start by remembering that, you can't go far wrong."

I put on my rain jacket, pulled the hood up, but the fabric was too thin to block him out.

"Follow the money if you want to know how things operate. Follow the money and if that don't work follow the cocks."

I started humming—Prince, though I couldn't remember all the words, went *dah-dah-dahhing* instead.

"I would have killed for her. Damn near did once. And what did I get in return once we married? Two hundred pounds of lard."

I wanted to put my rod down, cover my ears with my hands. And I did put it down—but only because we were entering a bad stretch of rapids now, and the driftboat was bucking so much I had to hold on. In our eight miles of river, this was the only dangerous spot, with abrupt granite ledges and a current stiff with turbulence.

And yet even this wasn't enough to shut him up. I tried concentrating on squinting into the spray exploding over the bow into my face. For a moment it worked, his voice became part of the current, something I couldn't read or decipher but merely had to ride. But then, in a calm spot between ledges, I heard him all too clearly, all too well.

"Love, right? Marriage, right? You get to smell their shit and listen to them pee, that's all marriage is my friend."

It was the tipping point, in every sense of the phrase. I stood up as if to jump overboard, then suddenly shifted my weight to the left, the worst possible thing I could do given our circumstances. Eli yanked hard on the oar and threw himself sideways, but too late. The gunwale dipped, righted itself, then dipped again, allowing the river to flood into the boat. Even then it didn't seem we would be swamped, but the bow smashed a rock, and, floating broadside now, the current had us at its mercy and threw us both out.

You hear about waders dragging people under, but mine tightened on my chest and gave enough buoyancy I didn't sink very deep. I was underwater for probably no more than twenty seconds, just enough to feel a great cleansing wash of exhilaration, as if I'd been scrubbed in a cold champagne bath. There was fear mixed in, most definitely there was fear, but I had always been a good swimmer, and I knew it was just a question of calmly riding the rapids out.

The confidence allowed me to enjoy it, in a strange kind of way. The bubbles especially. I had just enough lucidity, as they popped against my face, to understand that this is what a trout must experience, rising from the bottom to a floating fly. Sure, a hook was waiting in the end, but in the meantime, what a joyous and hopeful ride it must be.

That was for the first few seconds. I tried standing up, and though my boots scraped bottom the current tumbled me over again and it was another 50 yards before I gained purchase. Somewhere in all this I remembered Eli, had time to wonder if he could swim as well as I could—or could he even swim at all? Just as I got up, I saw him, or at least the limp gray wad the current made of him. He didn't seem to be trying very hard to stand up.

But this was an illusion, his passivity. Floating past me, about to disappear downriver, something brown shot out from the sodden ball of fabric, and my hand, lunging instinctively, met his hand and grabbed. We both grabbed— me to save him, him to be saved. I yanked and shoved until I had him upstream of me and the current could only bring him against my hips, not sweep him away. Staggering, my arms under his shoulders, I pulled him into the shallows and we both collapsed.

Late forties I had guessed for his age, but his time under- water seemed to have turned the stubble on his chin white, and his hair was matted like wet cat fur down over his nose. His eyes were closed, but he was breathing normally now, and the only thing I could find wrong with him was a jagged red slash across the lobe of one ear.

"What happened there?"

He reached and touched it, though even as I asked I realized it was scar tissue that had been there a long time.

"Arab kids. Bigger than me. Faster, too."

We stumbled the rest of the way to the bank, pulled our waders down, dumped out the river. Eli looked like a man who had just had his world view confirmed in spades, but I couldn't take it seriously anymore. Caught in the rapids, offered his ticket out, he had grabbed my hand, grabbed hard.

"Look," I said, pointing downstream.

The driftboat had come to a stop on the edge of a

sandbar. It lay low and heavy in the water, and, feeling guilty, I volunteered to go bail. When I got back, Eli was squatting on his heels beside a driftwood fire he'd lit with his lighter. It was almost dark now. When I followed the sparks skyward one of them didn't cool out like the others but became fixed in the direction of Emigrant Peak.

"Jupiter," I said, pointing. Then, before he could ruin it, I said what I thought.

"So, here's what we've discovered, using all those expensive satellites and telescopes. A lot of stars aren't solitary after all, but lie at the center of solar systems very similar to ours. They have planets—some are the size of earth. We've identified dozens of these, but eventually we'll find thousands, millions. Some of them, if they have this, will certainly know life."

I reached, dipped my hand in the river, let the water flow down my wrist.

"And they have to be just the right distance from their sun. Too close and they fry. Too far and they freeze. We're calling what lies in between the Zone of Habitability."

At first I didn't think he heard me, so intently did he stare at the flames.

"A planet like this one?" he finally said, screwing up an eye. "Same exact thing?"

"Sure. Maybe. Why not."

"Another earth?"

He pursed his lips with that, snapped his head down to spit into the fire.

"*Ebn el sharmoota!*"

I looked it up on my phone later. It means what you think.

# THE CALL OF THE WILD

Big things never defeated my mother, but against small worries she was defenseless. And so the growing pile of books on the dining room table, piled in two towers bridged by the oversized *Yuletide Customs of Many Lands*, seemed to her an insurmountable problem, with the library closing at five for Christmas Eve and her shift at the hospital not ending until seven.

As she readied breakfast, tried dressing me at the same time, she kept breaking away to go over to the table and stare at the books in dismay, poking at their spines with her thumb, biting her lip the way she did when making intense calculations in her head. The library would be closed for two weeks for vacation. There were 36 books on the table, some of them one-weekers. At ten cents a day for overdues that would mean $50 in fines by the time they were returned—a lot of money in a small mining town lost in the Montana north. The library did not have a book drop; our librarian believed in personally inspecting all returns for cracks, pencil marks, and blemishes—our librarian who was named, really named, Miss Agnes P. Crabtree.

"I could call Edna, ask her," my mother said, reaching for the phone. Then, just as suddenly, she put it down, remembering all the favors she'd already asked in that direction. She frowned, drummed her long, quick fingers against the table. "Or I could pile them on the front steps on my way downtown."

Alone at the table, Jackson not yet up, I took on his role as the family realist. "She'll slaughter you if you do that," I said. "It's supposed to snow more and they'll get soaked."

This was 1971—people were being arrested for overdue books all over the country, and my mother had made a point of reading those articles out loud every time one appeared. It was exactly the kind of thing she worried about. Here she was supporting a girl of eleven, a boy of thirteen, my father having left us and then almost immediately died in a logging accident—here she was, working long shifts as a nurse, dealing with our needs, coping with loneliness, doing all these well, without scars, at least not ones she let us see. But maybe that's what those smaller worries were, the bitter little pustules sent up by things too large for a child to sense.

"I could ask for an extension," she said, pinning on her nurse's cap with the careful, precise gestures I loved. "It's Christmas, after all. People are supposed to be charitous."

I frowned. "Ask her? Ask Miss Crabapple?"

"Crab*tree*. Well, I suppose Jackson could take them when he wakes up. But no, not in the snow. I could call Tom Bender, but I'd hate to owe him a favor."

That interested me. I sensed real substance to her worry now, not just the usual gnats. "Why not?" I asked.

"Never mind. I'll call you from work with the solution. I'll call you from work at eleven with the proper solution."

Cap on, coat wrapped around her shoulders, purse in hand, our old Ford warming up outside in a series of explosions loud enough to rattle the window glass and set the balls swaying on our tree, she still found it difficult to leave.

"In case anyone calls from the library, tell them—" She looked out the window at the gray sky, glanced down at the books again, seemed to lose heart at their number. "Tell them we're not home. Same if anyone comes with a warrant."

"A warrant?"

I pulled away from her hug. "Charitous isn't a word," I said, but by then she was already out the door, my little puff of defiance leaking out with her into the cold.

With her gone, I felt shy of the books and kept my distance. What confused me was how solid they looked and yet how fragile. I felt like I could stand with a foot on each tower and they would support any wild gyration I made, but if I breathed on them too hard they would all vanish into dust.

I was patting the bindings of the lowest books, trying to nudge them into alignment without the whole pile crashing down, when I heard a soft, cricket kind of noise on the bare spot where the rug ended, and turned to see Jackson standing there watching me, a toothbrush dangling from his lips like a purple cigarette.

He was already dressed, his wool checkered coat on, the coat that was far too small. He was going through a growth spurt, and everything about him seemed new and uncomfortable, so he was always reaching and tugging on himself—elbows, wrists, eyebrows—as if to pull the inner him up tight to the outer.

His mood had changed, too, in the months since our father left. A hardening had gone on, not so much in his own manner, but in his understanding of how the outside world worked. There were no overt symptoms of this, other than his going outside in winter to throw a baseball off the roof of our fallen-in garage, day and night, the thump-thump-thump of the ball down the shingles punctuating every other sound, until the last tinny beat when the ball hit the gutter, skipped once, then plopped into his out-stretched glove.

He had the glove with him now, brown and secret, pressed under his arm. Seeing this, I started right in on him, knowing I had only a few seconds in which to convert him to my cause.

"Mom said no going outside. You're to see the tree has water, then string up the twinkle lights. Tuna for lunch, but tonight's Swanson's potpies. I know where the presents are, but I'm not telling. She wants you to nail the mailbox back up in case we get more cards. We're supposed to get sixteen and a half inches of snow today. I have the best idea I ever had in my entire life."

I don't think he even heard me—all his attention was fixed on the books. His lips moved—was he counting? He hated any sign of incompetence on our mother's part, that frivolous, scatterbrained side of her, and, trying to see through his eyes, the twin piles of books certainly seemed frivolous.

Me, I was waiting for my favorite trick, which was him taking the toothbrush out of his mouth and using it to paste back the stiff blond bristles of his hair. But this is not what he did. He stared, sensed the fragile instability I had sensed myself, the way the book towers leaned. He tightened his hand into a fist, jutted his arm out karate style, swung it sideways through the bottom of both piles, collapsing them, sending books flying every which way . . . and it happened so fast, so suddenly, he was disappearing out the door even before the echoing boom of them had been absorbed and smothered by the rug.

"Jackson!" I yelled, far too late.

I picked the books up, frightened, angry, and yet my tidiness had an object now, and putting the 36 books flat on the table gave my intention time to harden.

There was a sled outside in the garage—a toboggan, we called it, though it was only a flyer with the runners rusted off. If I could find a way to fasten the books on top, I could probably pull their weight. The library was on the other, hilly side of town, but I had walked there once before—in summer. It should be entirely possible, even without my brother's help, to sled the books to the library, return them safely to Miss Crabtree's stern care, then race back in time to be home by dark, get supper started, light the tree.

I had no other Christmas presents for mother, other than drugstore perfume. The rightness of it caused tears to form in the corners of my eyes, and they only made my inspiration shine all the brighter.

In the downstairs closet, banished there when my father left, were two wool blankets he had saved from the army. I spread them out on the floor, laid eighteen books on one, eighteen books on the other, then tied their corners up with pins like giant diapers. There was twine left from wrapping presents, and I used it to make extra knots.

I dragged each bundle to the door, used my foot to push them out onto our stubby excuse of a covered porch. Next I grabbed my coat, stuffed two scarves under the middle where the zipper had broken, then, turning around once more to make sure I hadn't forgotten any books, pressed my way out the door into the heavy steel thickness of the day.

In other parts of the world, maybe even in other parts of Montana, the snow came down like it was supposed to, vertically, from a fluffy white pillow. In our town, set at the base of steep mountains, we never saw snow that wasn't horizontal—cold BB pellets that whizzed by so fast they made me blink. I watched for a moment, shivered more than I had to, tucked my head into my shoulders, and ventured forth, bending my body into the crouching stoop that was the default winter posture of everyone in town.

The sled stood propped against our coal bin as a kind of inner roof, catching what snow the dilapidated shingles missed. I pulled it down, dusted it off, brought it outside where I could see better. The runners were gone, but it was flat and surprisingly wide, and for a rope it had twin rubber fan belts my father had rigged as a harness.

After dragging it back to the porch, I slid the books down the steps onto its back, one bundle sticking out past the chevroned tail, the other by the rusty steering bar. I had brought more twine, scissors. I wrapped a long piece around the first bundle, weaved it back again, made three more turns around the sled's middle, tied twelve half-hitches, shoved on the sides as a test, nestled the fan belts against my shoulders, took three sharp breaths for good luck, started off.

Our street dropped down to the abandoned, shabby end of Main Street, but I couldn't go very far along this without hitting the railroad and an impassable trestle. I would have to take Jefferson Avenue instead, go three blocks east, then loop back to Main and start climbing until I reached downtown. Even here it would be difficult. The library was on Wheeler Street, but there was a confusing warren of smaller streets leading up to it, old cattle paths that had been paved without bothering to straighten them.

The storm had a copper smell—I remember that part. I was doing okay with the sled until I lost the protection of the houses and the wind hit me straight on. This made things harder, much harder. Leaving home, I'd been boosted by gravity, but now I hit a wall, one that didn't just stand there but jumped on me and slapped my face. The sled, so light on the downgrade, now seemed to weigh double, and the harness bit into my shoulder, squeezing off my circulation so my hands went numb under my gloves.

The railroad tracks pinched in here, so there were few house and no stores. The ranchers didn't like to bother with the downtown parking meters, so there were already lots of pickups lined against the curbs, families in to finish off their Christmas shopping before the snow cut off the back roads. I would pick out a red truck as target, decide I would pull that far and rest, reach it, feel satisfied, when a passenger door would fly open right in front of me, a whole family exploding outward into the snow, buttoning each other up, starting off quickly toward town, their heads bent into their chests like mine was, but having each other for windbreak and general support.

I was making good progress until I came to a river of slush flowing under the railroad ties, oozing down the embankment, fanning out across the street. What I should have done was unload the sled, carry the books one by one to dry ground. What I actually did do was give in to the stubborn streak in me, the part that was always in such a rush to do right it often led wrong. I heaved the sled to the side to free it of crust, tightened up on the harness, set off straight through the middle, deepest part of the slush.

I almost made it. The slush came up to the top of the sled but no higher, and I only had another ten feet to go when the worn nubble of the runners hit an unseen pothole, tipped downward, stuck, then, at my desperate tugging, plunged deeper, giving the sled such a violent cartwheeling motion the two bundles toppled overboard in matching fountains of syrupy gray slush.

Grabbing furiously, I pulled both bundles to safety, then went back and rescued the sled. The good news was that only the bottom of the blankets had gotten wet, but this was bad enough, since it made the bundles much heavier, and I couldn't be sure the wetness hadn't soaked into the books themselves. Worse, my splashing had gotten slush down the tops of my boots, and I could already feel it turning to ice water as it hit the warmth of my toes.

After tying things up again, feeling a premonition, I looked nervously around. There high on the railroad embankment, silhouetted against the sky like an Indian scout on a sandstone butte, stood Willard Hickey beside the flashy chrome of a brand-new bike—Willard Hickey, the mine owner's son, who was the last person in town I wanted to be seen by, not then, not ever. He watched me in silence, then disappeared down the other side of the embankment, all of this happening so fast and so quietly it allowed me to pretend it hadn't happened at all.

It was just then, as I manhandled the sled onto the dry, freshly-packed crust, that the dog sprang from the bushes and attacked. I screamed, first in fear, then in anger, kicking and flailing my arms about in an attempt to scare him back. It was the schnauzer that belonged to the missionary fathers who preached to the Blackfeet—a schnauzer infamous for irrational meanness and vicious intent. Having missed my ankles on his first pass, he rushed me again, shaking and snapping, his goateed muzzle covered in yellow froth. I yelled again, kicked snow, but all that did was make him switch targets from me to the sled. Something about it infuriated him, and he bit into the blanket and worried it with a frantic shaking until the fabric tore and the books spilled out onto the snow.

"Rollo!" one of the fathers called from off in the distance, sweetly, like he was calling in a bird.

The dog ran off, leaving me shaken, not so much at my own danger but at what he had done to my bundle. I had to start all over again tying it up; worse, the blanket had a hole in it now, and I wasn't sure it would keep the snow off if the storm intensified.

It was noon. I heard the church bells ring, then the whistle at the mine shaft beyond town. I thought of the sandwiches wrapped in cellophane back at home, scolded myself for not bringing one. There was starting to be enough traffic that it forced me to the inside of the street where the going was bumpier, and I had to keep looking over my shoulder to make sure I didn't get hit.

There had never been much enthusiasm for parks in our town or public spaces, but then someone got the notion that a ball field would be a good idea, and the mine owners had been persuaded to donate an old siding just off Main Street. In winter, it was flooded for ice skating, and this was what offered itself to me now: a smooth level surface where the sled would be much easier to pull than on gritty pavement. I detoured over, taking small steps so my boots wouldn't slip, eyeing warily a group of bundled-up hockey players slapping pucks toward the drifts at the pond's far end.

I was almost all the way across the ice, making much better time than I had made before, when someone missed a pass and the puck slid by in front of me, with six or seven players in pursuit. I don't think they would have bothered with me if not for the fact that at this same exact moment Willard Hickey appeared again on his bike, skidding to a spectacular stop on the ice right in front of me, his legs spread for balance, grinning in a way that made me think of Rollo the schnauzer with his teeth barred.

Willard Hickey was angelic looking, the teacher's pet, which made his darkness, his refusal to be anything other than mean, all the more confusing, at least to most people. To me, it wasn't surprising at all. Smaller than he was, always staring up at him from below, I noticed now what I had noticed before, extending across his scarf: the pale, sloppy underside of his chin. It was stretched and wrinkled at the same time, the skin of an old man, and it stuck forward like a shelf underlining his meanness and probably accounting for it. How could you help being mean with an underchin like that?

He didn't say anything to me directly—this was not Willard's way. He stopped the puck with his foot, waited until the hockey players braked, eyed them, made sure of them, then tilted his head toward where I stood shivering by the sled.

The oldest, stockiest of the boys immediately bent down to tear into the first bundle. What could he have expected to find there—Christmas presents? What he did find surprised him, and he held one up to show his friends. "Books!" he yelled, in derision and contempt. He flipped it to one of his friends who tossed it to one of the other boys who dropped it on the ice and swiped at it with his stick.

I knew what book it was, the smallest: *Everyday Thoughts for Everyday Courage*. It had been on my mother's bedside table for a month, and here they were hacking away at it, chopping at the cover, determined to knock it all apart.

They skated away with it up the ice, then swooped back again, the better to enjoy my torment. Willard took no active part, but stood motionless and unsmiling beside the show-off redness of his brand-new bike—and yet, through a means I didn't understand, he managed to communicate to the hockey players his commands.

Sensing this, the smallest of the boys, wanting to prove himself, dropped his stick and fell on the second, untouched bundle, ripping it apart, tossing books every which way on the ice. "Give me those!" I shouted, but of course this only inflamed them, and they started passing the books back and forth, whacking the smaller ones with cheerful ill-will.

There was a hole in the ice by the middle of the pond. They were steering the books in that direction, making it clear what would happen once they got them there, when there was a blurred motion to our left, a shape gliding toward us with the wind at its back, so it seemed a harder, more condensed version of the snow . . . and then gliding to a stop right in front of the hole, holding up his hand to desist like a comic book hero, was Jackson, my brother, my savior, appearing out of nowhere and appearing just in time.

It was hard to say who was more surprised, me or the hockey players. Jackson didn't bother saying anything to them, but went right over to Willard, stood there staring up at him, a foot shorter and yet taller in some unmeasurable moral way. A comic book hero would have jabbed out his arm and punched him, but this was not what Jackson did. He put his arm out all right, reached until his hand was just under Willard's chin, then lightly tapped him there—once, twice, three times.

With that came the second-biggest surprise of the day: Willard dissolved into tears.

He threw his hands up across his eyes, groped blindly for his bike, pedaled frantically off toward town, the wheels spinning up a spray of ice shavings that made his retreat look smoking. Their leader gone, the hockey players high-tailed it, too, and we were alone on the ice near the litter of the assaulted books.

Jackson's face showed no emotion, other than a little tightness in the lip area that could either have come from frowning or holding back a grin. Rescued, I felt shy in a way I'd never felt before, and blurted out the first thing that came to mind.

"You ran out on me, Stupid."

Jackson did frown this time—it was like he was trying to roll his icy lip over so the warm side would be out. "So?" he said, shrugging. "You're not allowed downtown either."

"I'm returning Mom's books to the library. Come on, help me pull."

He waved his hand around in a tight little circle. "See you later, Anna Franna."

For a change, I used my head. Jackson could face down bullies until the cows came home, but public embarrassment was another matter—he was morbidly sensitive about that. I bent down over the books until I found the exact one I wanted, opened it to the first page, started reading in the loudest, most obnoxious voice I could manage.

"Buck did not read the newspapers, or he would have known that trouble was brewing, not alone for himself, but for every tidewater dog, strong of muscles and with warm, long hair, from Puget Sound to San Diego."

I glanced up just long enough to check Jackson's reaction. He was forcing his fist into his ear, looking nervously over his shoulder to see if anyone could hear.

"Because men," I read, even louder, "groping in the Arctic darkness, had found a yellow metal, and because steamships and transportation companies were booming the find, thousands of men were rushing to the northland. These men wanted dogs, and the dogs they wanted were heavy dogs, with strong muscles by which to toil, and furry coats to protect them from frost."

Jackson bent down to see which book I read from. I snapped it shut, just missing his nose.

"Quit it!" he demanded.

"No! I'm going to stand reading here all day long. Louder than that, too."

Jackson knew I wasn't bluffing. I could see him considering the implications of being related to someone so publicly insane.

"All right. I'll help you pull. Town garage, no further."

"Library."

"Garage."

I sucked in more air. "Buck lived at a big house in the sun-kissed Santa Clara Valley. Judge Miller's place it was called. It stood back from the road, half-hidden—"

"Okay, okay! Library. But keep your trap shut and let's do it fast."

He helped me pile the books back on the sled. They didn't seem to be damaged other than some snow on their bindings, and this was easy enough to brush off. Jackson was good at tying knots, and so the load looked a lot more secure now. I put one fan belt around my shoulder, he put the other around his, and we started off, trying to match each other's strides so as to keep an even pull.

That close to downtown the traffic became more of a problem, and our sled couldn't have been easy to spot in the swirling gray snow. Cars already had their lights on, and we got honked at every time the beams caught our parkas. The merchants had wanted a Main Street worth bragging about, and to get it the buildings were flattened back against the bluffs, so it always made you think of a town being forced to stand taller and prouder than it really was. Set way back, the stores and banks presented no obstacle to the windblown snow—people walked faster, more stooped over here than anywhere else in town.

Jackson and I kept to the lower edge of the sidewalk, not saying much, concentrating on keeping the sled going at a steady pace. I was proud of that silence, enormously proud. Jackson said I was a chatterbox, someone who talked just for the sake of hearing herself talk, which was nearly the worst thing you could say of someone in the Montana of those years. But all that was frozen out of me that day. You couldn't utter anything in a wind so cruel, couldn't launch a word into that snowstorm unless it carried, seriousness, sharpness, and weight.

Jackson, for his part, seemed excited to be in town, and he stared at the Christmas lights and shoppes in a way that combined curiosity, envy, and pride. Here he was the strongest boy in eighth grade, the best athlete, the one who took the most risks, and yet that didn't mean anything now, he was as anonymous in the snow as I was, and I could see this was something he struggled against, his own private storm.

Main Street started climbing here, he had to hunch his back to pull, and that caused his right shoulder to go up, making me think of the description I'd heard applied to him so many times: *He has a chip on his shoulder, that one.* I remember thinking, he does have a chip, and it's a dangerous one, and I wish for his sake he would let it drop.

Pulling uphill made me sweat and the sweat made me shiver. Jackson made his face go all disgusted, but at the same time looked around for a place to rest. Where the hill flattened was an old station, abandoned now, ours being one of the first towns dropped by the Great Northern when passenger service began its long decline. The waiting room was padlocked, but between it and the ticket booth was a narrow alley where at least we would be out of the wind. I scrunched myself in, made room for Jackson, who wedged the sled in crossways so it was like we were tucked in an igloo the storm couldn't penetrate.

Jackson reached over to the sled, stuck his hand under the blanket, rummaged around like in a grab bag, brought it back out with a book.

"Why does Mom get all these?" he asked, genuinely puzzled.

Instead of answering, I looked down at the cover. It showed a beautiful girl with short black hair, and behind her inside a pattern of Valentines, a handsome boy in an argyle sweater.

"*Love Story.*"

"What's that?" Jackson asked.

I squinted down. "A blockbuster."

"Blockbuster?" Jackson hugged his knees to his chest, like the word alone made him warmer. "Kaboom," he said softly, blowing out his cheeks.

He handed me another book. "*Her Gracious Majesty,*" I read. "*The Life Story of Queen Elizabeth the Second.*"

"Yeah? Well, if she's the *second*, what happened to the *first*?"

We were in a routine now—him handing me books, me dusting the snow off, reading out loud their titles, Jackson making a little joke before putting them back under the blanket. There was *Boys Into Men: How to Raise Your Adolescent Son, Beauty Begins at Thirty-nine, Please Don't Eat the Daisies, Cooking Better For Less, Facing Bereavement Alone, Albert Schweitzer Doctor and Saint,* and some odder ones, titles I couldn't pronounce without giggling.

"*I Married Adventure.*"

"Who?"

"*I Married Adventure.*"

Jackson didn't laugh the way I expected, but looked serious, stern even, not much different that the way he had looked when he stared down Willard Hickey.

"What's the one you were reading from before?" he asked.

I scooted over on my knees to the first bundle, turned through the books until I found it. "*The Call of the Wild*. It's by Jack London who is famous." I thought for a second. "His real name was Jackson."

My mother's library books always included one she took out in the forlorn hope it would interest a boy; she was convinced that by merely leaving *Kidnapped*, *Tom Sawyer*, or *20,000 Leagues Under the Sea* on the dining room table, the magic would somehow kick in.

"Say that again," Jackson said, after a moment.

"*The Call of the Wild*. It's about this dog that goes to Alaska and has all these adventures in the gold rush."

I was about to say more when a gust more piercing than any other swirled snow into our igloo and brought with it a terrible premonition. I jumped up, went over to the sled, started frantically counting.

"Thirty-five! There's only thirty-five books here! One still must be back there on the hockey ice."

"So? We're returning most of them."

"Jackson!"

But he was already getting up, brushing the snow off his parka, squinting out to appraise conditions.

"You wait here," he ordered.

"It's almost dark. Watch our for cars."

"I'll walk on the tracks. It's faster."

There were still freight trains. "You'll be killed!"

I must have looked as frightened and lonely as I felt, because he hesitated now, his back to the wind so the snowflakes sprayed against his shoulders up toward his cap. "I married . . . disaster!" he yelled, cupping his hands around his mouth. That made me laugh, as he knew it would, and so it wasn't until it grew to totally dark out and he still hadn't come back that I began to get scared, this time for real.

The wind was so loud on the loose boards of the station I couldn't hear the church bells, and without them I lost track of time. Two men bundled in mackinaws sailed past on a handcar, pumping furiously—or did I imagine their shapes in the snow? The cold was the only thing that seemed definite—the kind of cold that attacks wrists, ankles, and toes, making me curl into a ball to try and escape. When that didn't work, I took the books and sat on them for insulation, then tucked some underneath my coat. And there was warmth there, that was the surprising thing. It was as if their pages exuded rays that surrounded my shivers, coated them, made them go still.

A train pushed by, and this time I wasn't dreaming. There was a yellow halo in the distance, then a rumble that made the platform shake, then the heady smell of diesel oil blurring past my nose. The train was the one force the storm was no match for, and it sent the flakes tumbling every which way trying to avoid the bluntness—and then it was gone, shrinking its way down the tracks. Where the blackness had been, just barely visible, came a small, stubborn shape dipping and bobbing as it strode from tie to tie.

"Got it," he said, before I could ask. He reached under his parka, pulled a paperback out, blew to get the snow off, held it up so I could see the cover: *Twenty-two Days to a Better You.*

"There's a chunk out of it!"

He nodded. "It was on the ice like you figured. Raven was picking at the pages. Damndest thing. Maybe it was salt or paste, the raven wanting salt."

"Miss Crabtree will kill us!"

This didn't scare Jackson, not after what he'd been through. "No she won't," he said quietly. "I won't let her."

He looked down the tracks the way he had come, took a deep breath like he was getting ready to tell me about his adventures, thought better of it, started beating his mittens together, then told me after all.

"The sled got caught in the tracks. There was this weird guy asking me if I wanted a ride. A power line was down shooting sparks I had to skip over. Mr. Daniel almost ran me over on account of he was driving with his arm around a blond. Aunt Edna stuck her nose up in the air outside Shroeder's and pretended not to see me. A smart guy laughed at me, gave me the finger, so I threw a snowball at him. There's a pretty little twelve gauge for sale in Anderson's window. I saw Tom Bender strutting bowlegged down Main Street acting important. It's snowing cinders further down. The weird guy drove back again and I ran. I couldn't hear the train in the wind until its light hit my legs and then I jumped."

I could see the rips in his pants, the cinders caught in the fabric, but none of this surprised me as much as the sheer velocity of what poured out. In that cold I had found silence—in that cold he found words. Finishing, marveling at himself with a little laugh, he pointed toward the dark.

"Let's get going."

There was no fooling myself now, not in that weather. "I can't. My toes are numb."

He considered this for maybe thirty seconds—it was the closest we came to giving up.

"You get up on the sled," he said at last. "I'll pull if you do something for me."

"What?" I said, immediately suspicious.

"You read out loud from that book while I'm pulling. The one you read from before. It makes it easier. You read, I pull."

I wedged myself on the sled between bundles, using one as a back rest, keeping the other between my legs. Jackson studied the arrangements with a critical frown, wrapped some twine over the spots that looked shaky, then looped the extra around my parka as a safety cord I could grab if I started slipping off. Satisfied, he put one fan belt around one shoulder, looped the other around his waist, tugged to the right to break the sled free of crust, dug his heels in, staggered, backpedaled, found purchase, started off.

He pulled across the railroad tracks, then swung left toward Wheeler Street, me sitting on the sled with the book open on my lap trying to read. The unlit street was totally deserted, and it was all I could do to find enough contrast to make out the words against the page.

"At Thirty Mile River one morning as they were harnessing up the team, Dolly who had never been conspicuous for anything, went suddenly mad. She announced her condition by a long, heartbreaking wolf howl that sent every dog bristling with fear, then sprang straight for Buck. He had never seen a dog go mad, nor did he have any reason to fear madness, yet he knew that here was horror and he fled away from it in panic. Straight away he raced, with Dolly, panting and foaming, one leap behind."

What light I had came from the snow; it blew from the direction of downtown and seemed to have absorbed extra energy there, iridescent flashes that made the words blink on and off across the page. Ahead of me, wrapped in a swarm of white pellets, Jackson slogged on, pulling harder now that we were going uphill. Wheeler Street was the oldest in town, the only one still cobblestoned, and the uneven rise and fall made pulling all but impossible. "Louder!" he shouted—and so I knew he was concentrating like I was concentrating, only with his ears, not his eyes.

"Dat Buck two devils," I read, making my voice go deep. "All de tam I watch dat Buck I know for sure. Lisen bygar. Some fine day heem get mad lak hell an' den chew dat Spitz up an' spit heem out on de snow. Sure I know, sacredam!"

I could see the library now, topping off the street like the Greek temple it was meant to resemble, the light yellowed up by its pillars, chopped into strips that slanted down-hill like ropes cast out to help us climb. It had to be five now—were we in time? The sled got stuck between cob-blestones, Jackson heaved, muttered, bent his body double, heaved again—and then we were breaking free, crossing the smooth flat surface that led to the steps.

"Hurry!" I shouted, but the strange thing was that now that we were arrived there neither of us could move. We felt intimidated, or at least I did—in awe of the fact we had made it, in terror that maybe it didn't matter.

The library looked deserted—there were no cars parked in front and no bootprints in the snow. *We're too late*, I was about to say, when high above us on the pillared entrance-way there was a clicking sound, a door opening and closing again, a dark shape moving swiftly out from the steps.

It was Miss Crabtree in a heavy wool coat, its collar folded high around her ears. She tested the door was locked, took one last appraising glance around to make sure all was secure, started lightly down the steps . . . saw us, stopped, placed one small white mitten over her heart.

"You startled me!"

She didn't look intimidating, not in that light, not up close. Her hair was jet black and worn short, and it framed an oval, delicately-featured face I knew was the kind my mother would like to have. I remembered now what I should have remembered before—that she wasn't mean at all, but only strict.

"We're returning some books," I said.

She looked down at the sled, looked over at us, then at the flattened track we had left in the snow.

"I can see that," she said at last. Then, remembering her duty, "Are they on time?"

I hesitated, took a deep breath, milked the moment for all it was worth.

"Yes. Every last one of them is on time."

She reached down to take the first bundle. "I'm all locked up, but we can put them on the portico."

It took us two trips, Miss Crabtree and I; Jackson hung back in the shadows. The portico was wrapped in burlap for insulation, and we made a pile of books near the door where the snow couldn't touch them.

"They're thirty-six of them," I told her, as she bent down to count.

"Thirty-five," she said, frowning.

I didn't believe her . . . I was kneeling down to count myself . . . when Jackson stepped out from the shadows with a book in his right hand.

"I want to take this one out again," he said softly. "There's a word for that, but I don't know what it is."

Miss Crabtree straightened up. "Renew?"

"I want to renew this."

I saw what book it was now—remembered leaving it open on the sled after I stopped reading. Miss Crabtree took it from him, glanced down at the title, smiled very briefly, then made herself look stern.

"Do you know what tonight is? It's Christmas Eve. I have a party to go to, my fiancé waiting. You can come back after vacation and take it out then. I can't open up after I've closed."

Jackson looked at her without flinching—his voice was quiet and firm.

"No. You're going to open this door and get your stamper pad out and renew this book."

Miss Crabtree sucked in her breath—I could see her getting ready to put him in his place—when she made the mistake of looking directly in his eyes. I couldn't see them myself, not from where I stood, but what was visible there must have been convincing past all possibility of doubt. She made a little nodding motion, then went and unlocked the library door.

I could see the two of them inside the window by the high mahogany desk, Miss Crabtree opening the book flat so she could stamp it, Jackson waiting patiently with his mittened hands behind his back. Finishing, she handed it over. As he came back through the yellow light that framed the door he was already reading, making a little boring in motion with his nose and chin as he pressed them close to the page.

I can see him now, doing this. There was a wild beautiful something in books those years. There was a wild beautiful something in my brother Jackson MacInnes. The world would break and tame it very quickly, but the deepest part of him, the inner terrain he began discovering in the course of that journey, it could never tame. What I remember about him is not the sadness that came later, but him climbing down those icy library steps in the dark of Christmas Eve, reading as he walked, the book outstretched before him at eye level, his shield against the snow.

But no, my memory needs sharpening here. It wasn't like a shield, the way he held it. He held it like a spear.

# TWO CHAIRS

WHO MADE THE DISCOVERY had always been their great debate—58 years hadn't been enough to settle it. The basics they agreed on. Their honeymoon. Not enough money for anywhere fancy. Tourist cabins a friend recommended upstate. On their last day there, taking a long drive along a country road of choppy macadam changing over to dirt. A sudden hissing noise, steam shooting out the radiator, pulling over, a ruptured hose, going over to a river to fetch water in his hat—and then, miraculously, the chairs.

"Why do you always remember it wrong?" Vera said from the passenger seat. "We had a flat tire, there was no spare, a farmer stopped on his tractor, said he'd get someone from the garage, and while you waited I decided to take a walk toward a stream we saw in the distance."

*I remember it wrong deliberately. I remember it wrong to tease you and to make a little joke when we tell the story to others and because arguing over details like this is half the fun of sharing memories that stretch back as far as ours. And besides, it was the hose.*

Only an hour to go now—they always began talking about the chairs with an hour to go. "Flat tire," Vera mumbled, and then her head fell back on the seat and she dozed. That was fine, she would arrive there rested, be able to greet Mr. Thompson with all her old vivacity, not give him cause to worry.

He was tired himself—no, bored. The billboards flying by, the assholes and bullies, the way the interstate slapped down the landscape and sat on its corpse. You could have your fill of these, after driving as many miles in his life as he had. When Vera was awake it was bearable, but when she slept, driving wearied him as it never had before. It was only by concentrating on the chairs, what they represented, that he was able to keep on.

One of the reasons they argued about how they found the chairs is that after finding them they agreed on every detail. The path had led through a meadow, with grass that was higher than their hips and luxuriously pliant. Finches flew up from their nests, bobolinks and meadowlarks. The black-eyed Susans were startling, their gold was so vivid, and further along the path they had to duck under a bower of wild raspberries fatter and redder than any they had ever seen.

Where this tunnel ended the path opened into a patch of wild grass bordering the river. It wasn't a wide or particularly deep river, and its color was a blend of emerald and mud. Willows grew from the banks, casting a tropic shade over the shallows—the river was high enough to stroke the lowest fronds. "The Nile!" Vera said. It was years before they learned the real name was Pig Creek.

As beautiful as the river was, it wasn't what made their

discovery remarkable, but what they found overlooking it in the center of the clearing. Two chairs. Two Adirondack chairs placed inches apart facing the water, though in those days no one called them Adirondack chairs, they were just the kind of wide-back wooden chairs you saw when you went north on vacations. These were homemade, with too many nails and faded red paint, but the roughness made them blend even better into the setting. It was as if they had been planted there as splinters, and had sprouted to maturity under the softening patina of the weather.

"It's like someone knew we were coming," Vera said, as they bashfully walked over. "Like they drew us here and invited us to sit down."

They felt like Hansel and Gretel approaching the gingerbread house in the middle of the forest. They reached out and touched the wood to convince themselves it was real, then, Gordon going first, plopped themselves down.

The chairs sagged under their weight, enough that they braced themselves for a crash, but it was only the wood's resiliency, and they quickly decided the chairs were the most comfortable they had ever sat in.

"Who put them here?' Vera wondered. "A farmer? We've driven quite a way and there's been no sign of a house."

Right from the start this was the great mystery—who had put the chairs out? There were two chairs, this was the only clue, and so they drew the obvious conclusion: that it was a couple who had brought the chairs there, probably a few years older than they were, a little ahead of them in life. Whoever they were valued peacefulness. Whoever they were enjoyed being with each other. Whoever they were loved  meadow grass, sunshine, water.

They talked about that, then, falling silent, stared out at the spreading semi-circles of the moving river. Like the chairs, it always puzzled them, no matter how familiar its brown-green color eventually became. Where did it originate? Where did it flow? The Nile was a good name, it had that kind of mystery, and they both sensed this right from the start.

"It's flowing toward China," he said, with a little nod.

"No," she said, after a minute of thought. "It's flowing to a place far beyond that."

The chairs were so comfortable it was hard forcing themselves to get up. Comical really, the way they said "Let's go now," then, half-rising, sank back again with contented sighs. Finally, Vera got up and walked over to the river, stood watching something in the shallows he couldn't see himself. She wore a peach-colored sundress, the kind that had never come back into fashion in all the years since, and the color matched perfectly the soft color of her tan.

He did get up now, walked over to join her. "Look there," she said, pointing toward the current, but he didn't look there, he took her in his arms, with all the tenderness he was capable of—and that was the real moment of their marriage, there was none of the awkwardness of their first time together, and in all the long years since, when he thought of their wedding, he remembered, not the drafty Methodist church it had happened in, not the half-senile preacher who went with it, but the river and the chairs and the two of them lying in the meadow grass in the sweet smell of sage.

Just when his fatigue was about to master him, they came to the exit and the last few winding miles of road. As always, he nearly missed the last turn—the signless last turn with the slow S of its hill, the welcoming coolness of the hemlocks, a collie, the latest in a long line, rising stiffly to its feet in greeting, and then the cabins, Thompson's Cabins, asleep as the dog had been, but much too lazy to stir into life.

There was no need to ask which cabin was theirs. Chippewa was theirs—it was furthest from the dining hall, but had the deepest shade. He dropped Vera off there, lugged in the heaviest of their bags, then went in search of Mr. Thompson.

Thompson's had changed little over the years, which was exactly its point. It had started life as a dozen shabby tourist cabins run by the original Thompson. Thompson junior, after serving in the Air Force, came back and turned the property into a bona-fide resort, though a modest, low-key one. The cabins were replaced by more comfortable versions made of logs hewn on the property—a tennis court was put in, a path cut down to the lake. Wisely, he had pretty much stopped at that, drew his customers from families who returned year after year just because it hadn't been modernized, so traditions built on it could last.

At Thompson's, small changes loomed large. Now, as he walked down the path toward the office cabin, he noted a new flower bed, a log bench near the tennis court, a new roof on the dining hall. *Must mention these to Mr. T.*, he told himself—he was hurt if guests didn't notice all the little improvements.

Mr. Thompson was outside Algonquin, nailing down a loose plank on the deck. "Was getting worried about you!" he said, rising stiffly like the collie, sticking out a pants-swiped hand. "You always arrive by three, set my clock to it, and here it's half-past five."

"Traffic," Gordon said, though he might just as well have said "Age."

Mr. Thompson was Mr. Thompson the Third and Gordon could remember the days when he had been a madcap twelve-year old on a rickety Schwinn bike. He had aged quickly after his father died. He had put on green work pants, a green work shirt, let his beard grow fuzzy, started in with a pipe. It had seem deliberate, calculated, as if crusty old coot was his destiny in life and he saw no reason for delay.

"So," he said, as they walked back toward the office. "How's the newspaper business treating you? A big-shot reporter, always on the go. They have you working on any murder stories?"

"I was circulation director. Retired, you know that. And glad I am, since papers are on the ropes right now, it's a dying profession."

"And Vera? Still training dogs for blind people?"

"She records talking books for the sightless. It's her voice, they were always asking her to do more. But she's retired now, too."

"Grandkids? Five of them, ain't it?"

"Flourishing. The youngest graduated from college in May, little Ted. Do you remember Ella, the tomboy redhead?"

"Luke's girl? What a tiger!"

"She's expecting our first great-grandchild in October." He looked toward the lake, as if that's where October lay. "Are the Bukowskis coming up this summer?"

Mr. Thompson shook his head. "Hip's gone. Hers, too."

"Hips are tough. Well, how about the Thurstons?"

"She died, you didn't get a card?"

"The Marinos?"

"Don't ask."

"Bob and Elsie?"

"Nothing. No word. Nope."

He tried a few more names, but they only produced the same kind of litany—and then Mr. Thompson started complaining about gas prices, what they were doing to his business.

"Chippewa okay for you?" he said, shaking off the mood. "Always can upgrade to Iroquois if you feel like more elbow room."

"It's fine, absolutely perfect just as ever." Gordon hesitated, then brought out the words he'd spent the last few minutes rehearsing.

"Do you remember the time Luke got caught in the poison ivy and we took him to the hospital? That time when Melissa cut her hand on the dock and we took her there for stitches?"

Mr. Thompson gave his beard his pensive, old-coot scratch. "Dad hated that poison ivy, went to war on it with a flamethrower."

"Is that little hospital still there?"

"County Central? It's still there—if you're desperate."

"And if you ever call 911 for any reason, is it them that will come?"

"Them or the fast squad."

The office phone rang, and Gordon assumed he had managed to slip it by him after all. But then, walking up the hill to Chippewa, Mr. Thompson took his arm, made him stop.

"How's Vera?"

"Vera's fine," he said, after a pause. "Come see for yourself, she'll be thrilled to see you."

They had wanted to come back to celebrate their first anniversary, but he was just starting his career, working impossible hours, she had taken a temporary job in a store, and they couldn't find the time or money to make the trip north. The summer after that they were going to try someplace more adventurous, but money was still tight, and even a week at Thompson's seemed like an extravagance. "Let's go back to see if the chairs are still there," she said, and that settled it. Their week turned out to be perfect—he taught her how to fly fish; she helped him on his tennis— and it wasn't until their next-to-last day there that they went in search of the chairs.

It was confusing, at least at first, since the dirt part of the road had been smoothed and re-routed. But he was good with things like that, he recognized the pull-off, and parked where the path parted back the grass. They all but ran toward the river, the Nile. It was higher than the first time, so far up the banks that wildflowers bobbed on the surface, and the current, rather than just whispering, gurgled, babbled, and cooed.

"Three chairs!" she said, racing ahead of him, stopping to point. "Goldilocks and the three bears!"

The new chair was half the size of the other two, made out of the same rough-cut wood, only with redder, fresher paint. It was set protectively between the two larger chairs, and it was impossible to look at it without drawing the obvious conclusion.

"They have a baby now," he said. "Whoever they are,

they're parents, good for them." He rapped his knuckles on the chair backs.

"Congratulations, whoever you are."

Vera crossed over to the small one, rocked it gently back and forth. "Whoever you are," she said, lulling the words into a little song.

"They love this spot. They have a little baby boy or girl. What else is there to know?"

The thing they noticed, then and later, was that the scene became even lovelier, more perfect, when they were sitting down watching, not standing up. It was a trick of perspective, or some magic in the chairs themselves, cradling them so gently that their sense of wonder opened up. The sun was bright on the water's surface, they had to shade their eyes to see, but never had he felt so strongly that they were sharing what they looked at—that their seeing, after the exhilarations and upsets of their first two years together, had now become one.

They were silent for a long time. "We're going to need three chairs, too," she said, very softly.

"Three?" He glanced over at her, not really getting it. "Yeah, someday I suppose."

"April ninth, if the doctor is right."

And he went nuts with that, the way every young man should go nuts when his wife finds a cute way to tell him. He jumped out of the chair and fell on his knees, taking her hand, kissing her, asking questions and making plans and asking more questions and making more plans, until she playfully pushed him away—and, a second later, reached toward him again and held him tighter than she ever had before.

•

And now this week, their fifty-third at Thompson's Cabins. They hadn't come back every year, but most years. After they established their careers, once the kids were old enough, they took trips to Europe and Montana and all the famous national parks, and then, retiring, they managed a trip to Alaska. But even in the years they traveled, they often managed to slip in a trip upstate, usually toward the end of August when the weather turned perfect.

They did their best with this latest week, their quiet best. Time had slowed a lot of things down, but not their walking, and the paths around the lake didn't seem noticeably steeper or more challenging than they had in the past. On Monday, with Vera experiencing one of her exhausted mornings, he went out in a rowboat alone, but it had been frustrating, since, with his vision, he couldn't thread the fishing line through the eye of the hook. He rowed around the shallows, staring down at the smug-looking bass, mad he couldn't catch them. It had taken a long nap in the shade, lying across the middle seat, to restore his temper.

Even when they were younger, reading had been the best part of their stay, and nothing stopped them now from indulging themselves all they wanted. All three Mr. Thompsons understood the merit of shade trees and hammocks, and that's where they spent most of their day, she with a book on France, he reading one on Gettysburg. At night, in the yellow twilight left in their cabin, she read out loud to him from an old favorite, Willa Cather's *My Antonia*.

Her voice was as musical as ever and nearly as strong. Listening, he pictured blind people listening to one of her talking books, understood how beautifully hypnotic the sound must have seemed to them, with its contralto richness, its measured preciseness tinged with a slightly dream quality, as if the words she was reading were extraordinarily special, the world they described even more special, existing in a realm that, unlike everything else in the world, time wouldn't dent.

"I can remember exactly how the country looked to me along the faint wagon tracks on that first September morning," she read, stretched out beside him on the cabin's sofa, his hand lightly on her knee. "More than anything, I felt motion in that landscape, in the fresh, easy-blowing wind, and in the earth itself, as if the shaggy grass were a sort of loose hide, and underneath it herds of wild buffalo were galloping, galloping."

How many sightless men, he sometimes wondered, had fallen in love with her through her voice? Listening in the darkness, they must have tried hard to visualize her looks, the way they tried picturing the prairie or steppe or moors described by her voice. If he was ever tempted to take her for granted, this little trick always snapped him out of it. *I can open my eyes and see her. I can reach out to her voice and kiss her on the throat.*

She fell asleep, reading. He found a quilt to tuck her in, then pulled a chair over to the bed where he could be near her if she needed him during the night. Always on these vacations he slept soundly, but the magic seemed gone now, and he lay awake listening to what sounds drifted up from the lake. Frogs. Water lapping against a dock. The hum of a trolling motor, some fisherman out late. Soft feminine giggles, followed by a splash.

These were the sounds which had always lulled him into sleep, but they couldn't do it this time, not against his anxiety. But no, anxiety wasn't quite the right word—what he felt was expectancy, though expectancy for what he couldn't quite say. It involved a sound and the sound could only come from where Vera lay sleeping, but he couldn't give it a name. A cry of pain? Yes, he would recognize that if it came. A cry of loneliness, of solitude and despair? Well, he would try his best with that, too. What despair would sound like he had no idea, but he listened anyway, and, listening, the softness of the water sounds slowly had their way with him, and he finally fell asleep.

It wasn't until their seventh or eighth visit that they absolutely trusted the chairs would be there. By then, Melissa and Luke were born, had reached the toddler stage, but that was okay, since there were four chairs there now, so they each had their own. The homemade wooden ones had given way to steel lawn chairs, surprisingly comfortable and springy—one was green, one was red, one was blue, one was lemon. They weren't there long, they must have rusted over the winter, because the next summer they found aluminum lawn chairs, with nylon mesh on the backs, and rounded tubes on the base that allowed you to rock back and forth.

Family traditions, family legends. With the years, they accumulated more than their share there. One year, a summer of drought, the Nile had been so low that Luke crossed the river hopping from sandbar to sandbar. He and Melissa had rock-skipping contests which Melissa always won. They once found a muskrat asleep on a log, and then an osprey swooped toward the river and came out holding a fish.

Caught in a thunderstorm, they turned the chairs upside down for shelter. A plastic baseball came bobbing down the current, followed five minutes later by a plastic bat. Their picnics grew simpler each year, until all they brought was lemonade, apples, and cheese.

Who owned the land, who put out the chairs, they never discovered, though they talked about "them" constantly. Each trip they expected to run into "them," rehearsed what they would say, became shy about it—how could they explain that they had been trespassing on their lives?

"Someday we'll meet them," Vera would say, when the afternoon was over and they started back down the path for another year.

"Well, we always come in the afternoon," Gordon said. "What if their habit is to come and watch the sunrise in the morning? We'd never see them. Same with sunsets. Or what if it's summer people and for some reason they're never up here during our week?"

In the early years, they made token efforts to find out who they were. The second Mr. Thompson devoted some time to it, even going so far as to look up property records at the county seat. There had been a farm there back in Civil War days, but it had long since been divided into separate fields, and while these fields had changed hands several times since, none of the maps showed any of the rectangles actually touching the river. It seemed that this particular meadow wasn't owned by anyone at all.

A mystery, certainly. Luke suggested leaving a message in a bottle, placing it underneath one of the chairs where the other family was bound to see it. They had a mayonnaise jar with their picnic, Vera scrubbed it out with sand, but when it came time to writing the message, none of them knew what to say.

Luke was seventeen now, Melissa one year younger—it was a miracle they still found enough fun at Thompson's to want to come back. As usual, they had left the visit for the river for their last full day. Luke and Melissa raced each other to get to the chairs first, and Gordon and Vera were unpacking their picnic from the car when they heard two loud and startled shouts.

When they reached the meadow they found Luke spinning around and around like someone who had dropped his wallet, and Melissa spinning the opposite way, as if she had lost one of her contacts. Vera understood before he did. She stopped, nodded, pointed—and then he understood, too. There were three chairs in the meadow. Not four chairs. Three.

"One of their kids has grown up now and left home," Vera said. "Maybe to college, or a job in another part of the country. They only have one child living with them now, not two."

A simple enough deduction—why did it hit them so hard? Melissa and Luke were already over by the river for the latest renewal of their rock-skipping contest, and Gordon and Vera watched them tease each other and laugh, feeling all the while that time and its changes were thumping them painfully on the back. The next year, Luke was in college, and the year after that Melissa went, too, and Vera had to tell them via postcards that, when they got to the meadow that year, the three chairs were now down to two.

So, full circle. The two chairs looked small and forlorn set in what suddenly seemed an empty, lifeless meadow—but this phase didn't las very long. After a few years, having just the two chairs there seemed the most natural thing in the world, and it was hard to remember a time where there were three chairs, let alone four. One year, the aluminum lawn chairs were replaced by the kind of old wicker chairs you might find at a yard sale, but then a few years later these were replaced in turn by beautifully crafted, exquisitely varnished Adirondack chairs the couple must have bought themselves as an extravagant present, possibly for an anniversary, very probably their fiftieth.

With just the two chairs being there now, they started a new tradition: neither one of them was allowed to talk while they were sitting down. Walking the path, going over to the river, turning through the wild apples to see whether any were ripe—doing these, they could chatter away all they wanted, but once they sat down in the chairs they had to be completely silent, watching the water together, sharing the same sensations, but never never saying a word.

"Here we are, sitting in our epilogue," Vera said once, breaking their rule.

He squeezed her hand. "How long do epilogues last?"

She squinted toward the palette-shaped clouds, seemed to give the matter real thought, but then, remembering their rule again, she put her finger to her lips and smiled.

Their week ended on Friday, which meant Thursday was the day for the chairs. On Monday night, thinking she had fallen asleep after reading, going over to cover her with the quilt, he was surprised to see her eyes were still wide open.

"Okay?" he asked.

"No," she said, to the wall more than to him.

"Pain?"

"No." She twisted around, reached her hands out to him, managed with his help to sit up. "Something is different, but I can't give it a name. I've been trying, and I can't, it's too deep inside. But I think we better go home early."

"We'll go home tomorrow."

She squeezed her eyes shut, struggled to open them again. "No—Thursday. We can stay until then. It's enough."

"Enough?" he said. The word jumped out on its own—he knew full well what she meant.

In the morning he went in search of Mr. Thompson to tell him about their change in plans. He hadn't been around much during the week, and only now did it occur to Gordon that he might be deliberately avoiding him. When he did find him, it was outside the shed used to store kayaks and bikes. He had on brand-new work clothes, which made him look green and stiff.

"I need to talk to you," Gordon said.

Mr. Thompson gravely nodded. "Figured you'd find out. A reporter like you, an old newshound. I've decided to sell. The offer is a fair one and I thought it was time to say yes."

"Sell the cabins?"

"And the land. I think it's time. With my guests—"

"Dying off?"

Mr. Thompson shot him a look. "Getting older, I thought it was time. There's an assisted living community for seniors looking for a site, and they like the idea of being near a lake. I wouldn't sell to just anyone. Nothing's final yet. But it's pretty close to final. I wouldn't do it unless they reserve units for my regulars, so they can move up here permanently."

This is what Gordon was fighting as he walked to the dining hall to meet Vera—the fatigue that came with a lifetime of seeing change always win. A sanatorium, a golf resort, a water slide park, a rustic mall. Their possibility loomed on the horizon for a summer or two, cast their baleful shadow, then somehow dissolved. Senior assisted living, he suspected, would not dissolve. It was the triumph of demographics, and he was personally to blame, merely by adding one wretched digit to the exploding total of those who were old.

The good news was that by Thursday Vera felt stronger. Their tradition, on chair day, was to order pancakes for breakfast, and she surprised him by eating everything on her plate.

"Ready?" he asked, when they finished their coffee.

"Ready?" She smiled—it took possession of her face in a way it hadn't in a very long time. "Ready when you are Freddy. And I want to drive, please don't say no, because I always drive there, and you always drive back."

This had never been a problem before, but now maybe it was, since it gave him time, a little too much time, to think about things and brood. *Let's not go*, something strange in him wanted to say. It startled him, the words coming from nowhere and almost making it past his lips. *I can't say why, it's only a silly premonition, but it's real, and it's telling me we should immediately turn around.* Before he could find even the semblance of a possible excuse, Vera was pulling over to the sandy widening in the road where they always parked, and it was too late to say anything.

Vera, because she had led the way up the path the first time they had ever come, got to go first up the path every summer since, a rule even their grandkids respected back in the years when they came along, too. Now, though, she hesitated. There was a narrow border where the alders grew thick—it had always been necessary to search a bit before locating the opening—but instead of pushing her way confidently through them, she seemed to timidly shrink back.

"I can't find it," she said, with real despair.

Gordon hurried over. "It must be overgrown from all the rain. It's right about—here!"

He pulled some leaves back, kicked aside a dead branch, held open a hoop of vines. Wild blackberries lay coiled over the meadow grass and their thorns were treacherous, at least for the first few yards. Storms had brought down branches and limbs, which he had to stoop down and remove. They usually walked two abreast, hand in hand, but the path was so choked they had to keep single file. He helped her through a wet spot, let her go first through the border of ferns that marked the clearing, came out in the open next to her, stared into the sun.

One chair—fine. He squinted to make the second one out, but his eyes found nothing except a few top-heavy tassels of grass. He blinked, changed his angle slightly. One chair. He rubbed his eyes, adjusted his glasses, blinked again—but none of it mattered. There was only one chair.

It hit them so hard they stepped closer to each other, found hands, grabbed tight—he had just enough perspective left to think of Hansel and Gretel again, as he had their first time. Together, shyly, they took the few steps necessary to come up to the chair from the back. It was one of the beautiful wooden ones, glistening in the sunlight as if its varnish was still wet, but beside it was nothing but two groove-like scars in the meadow grass decorated with centipedes and worms.

One chair. There were so many implications it was exactly as if there were no implications at all, or not any he could wrap his mind around. Automatically, as if they were sitting down at a restaurant, he put his hands on the chair, rocked it slightly backwards. *You first*, the gesture said.

She shook her head. "You. You sit down."

"You need the rest."

"Please? You?"

Ludicrous, their little argument, and Vera was sensible enough to give in. She sat down, he kneeled on the grass beside her, then they both turned their heads simultaneously toward the Nile. This, at least, hadn't changed. The grass on the banks was starting to brown, but it still had the same pliancy as ever—it flowed the same direction the river did, mimicking its current.

They sat there silently, she in the chair, he next to her on the grass. There was so much to say, and so they said nothing, and besides, silence had been their rule, their tradition, for a good many years now.

A crow slanted across the sun, and it was this that finally stirred him. He walked over to the bank, found a branch to steady himself, stood staring down with his feet well braced. With the rain of the summer, the water was higher up the banks than he remembered it ever being, so the sun's rays skipped off the surface rather than penetrating. A dead tree trunk, gray with age, floated down the middle, and there was enough turbulence that it rolled over and over, faster than what you might expect given its size.

Why, he wondered, had he ever thought of the river as being placid? It disguised itself in placidity, pretended to be meandering and lazy, and now here it was in its true, unapologetic self, the guise it must wear in winter when they were many miles away. Unstoppable, that's how it looked. But why would a river ever want to stop?

Wryness would see him through, as it had for so many years now. But then, in turning back to the chair, he saw something that tore his agony right apart. Vera sat where he had left her, only now with something rigid in her posture—she gripped the arms of the chair with so much force her arms turned white. She pressed her head against the chair back, closed her eyes, making it seem as if she were on a spaceship experiencing several times the force of gravity. He hurried toward her, was about to call out, but then her body relaxed, her eyes opened, and she seemed as comfortable and relaxed in the chair as ever.

"I want you to come back next summer and sit here," she said, when he reached the chair. "I want you to do this for as many years as you can."

"No." He made sure she saw him, slowly shook his head. "Can't do that."

She smiled, took his hand, pressed it down on the armrest with hers so they shared one part of the chair at least. With her other hand she made a circling gesture, taking in the river and the meadow grass and the sky and the sun until it all mixed together in what, the motion ending, became her frail, very determined little fist.

"This is what forever looks like," she said, in the soft tone there was never any arguing with. "Fifty-eight years is forever, and so we see it as few are ever allowed to. We see it so clearly, so whole, that we know you can come out on the

other side and understand that even forever has an end . . .
I want you to come back next year and sit here without me.
If I'm not going to make a silly fool of myself with what's
going to happen, I need to know that you will."

*No, I can't do that. Not because of sadness, but because of
happiness. Because happiness is intolerable when it's looked back
upon alone.*

He tried shaking his head, but he didn't have enough
strength, looked instead back toward the river. The sunshine
was so strong he had to close his eyes against it, and when
he closed his eyes, he had, for the first time ever, a dis-
tinct vision of the couple who owned the chairs, the famous
"them."

But no, it wasn't "them" at all, but only the man, the
husband, the one he sensed very strongly must be the
survivor. He pictured someone four or five years older than
he was, venerable looking, dignified, walking with a slight
hunch in his shoulders, but nothing worse than what you
might see in a teenager, hardly enough to slow him down.

A tall man, at least in his prime. A watchful man, someone who was comfortable just looking out at the world, for
many hours at a time. Glasses, white hair, strong arms,
roughened hands, delicate fingers. A perspective that time
couldn't shrink or frighten. A man of courage, to be able to
make his way up the path and sit here alone. A man leading
the way for him. A man worth emulating.

He opened his eyes, turned slightly, saw the face he had
loved since he was a boy, looking expectantly up at him
waiting for an answer. *No, Vera, I can not come again*, he was
about to say to her. "Yes, I will come," is what the words
managed on their own.

# THE OLD CAMPAIGNER

Signs still matter in a small state like dad's. You can spend a fortune on TV ads, import all the lies and hatred money can buy, charm your way through the debates, but unless you plant campaign signs along the road or in people's yards, you don't have a prayer. Voters want to have a stake in you, Dad would say, laughing at the pun. His sign read *You're My Boss Vote Bob Lilly*, and he hadn't changed a word in the eleven consecutive elections he had won to the state senate.

It was surprising that he was running again—everyone who knew him was surprised. He's 78 now, with heart trouble in the background, and Mom, in her final illness last spring, had told him he'd done enough. But without the rock of their partnership he had trouble filling up his days, and it was probably too much to ask, giving up the two main pillars of his life all at once. And there was unfinished business he cared deeply about. Restoring funding for the handicapped after the previous senate had gutted it.

Preserving a big swath of forest up north where for many years he had run a summer camp. Keeping gambling casinos out of the state. He still felt capable of battle.

But first he had to get himself re-elected. Out went the signs, in the same roadside spots he had used for twenty-two years running. He was like a gardener in this respect. Seeing the signs gradually spread from the shoulders across the sidewalks onto people's lawns made him feel good about democracy.

His opponent was a car dealer from the bottom of the state named Lawrence Billings, a complete nonentity. Republican, he called himself, but it was more Tea Party than that. As with all his previous opponents, Dad was cordial to him, respectful, and, deep inside, absolutely convinced he would whip his butt.

I tried following all this from California, which was like following it from Mars. And I'd be lying if I didn't admit there was some tension between us. Dad was middle-of-the-road on politics, but old-school about family, and though he fought through this most of the time, I could sense his disapproval when I did things my way.

My job paid a lot more than Rick's, demanded much more of me, so it seemed sensible to let him raise Melissa while I concentrated on my career. Dad grew used to this, but then, in the course of things, it seemed silly to be commuting between San Jose and Sacramento, so even on weekends I stayed near work. That seemed stupid after a while, too, pretending I was still a mother, so, when Rick wanted to end things, I made no fuss about visitation.

Dad wasn't happy. And he didn't like my friends, the people I worked and played with—liked even less that he couldn't understand what exactly it was I did. It was sort of cute at first, parents being helpless with technology, having to tutor them, but that kind of thing stopped being funny nine or ten years ago.

I was deep in a new project during the summer, and if I gave the election any thought, I assumed he was coasting to victory. But then on Halloween I got a call from his old pal Peter Lahm that turned everything on its head.

Peter had been chief political reporter on a Concord newspaper for every one of Dad's campaigns, but then a national chain bought the paper, the chain closed it, and now, from habit, he followed the election as a blogger, unable to quit.

"Your Dad's in trouble," he told me. "Things have changed, and he doesn't understand that. The latest polls show him being trounced."

As I said, his opponent was a clown, but he was being coached on what to say. At town hall debates, instead of asking about taxes, roads, infrastructure, issues Dad was an expert on, ringers got up in the audience and asked him about foreign affairs and abortion and where he stood on guns. When it came his turn, Lawrence Billings—who had the decency to look embarrassed—referred to Dad as "Lilly Liberal," and that's basically all he said in the next month of campaigning. Lilly Liberal promises this, Lilly Liberal promises that. Every time he said it his poll numbers rose.

There was one town meeting in particular. A burly guy in a motorcycle jacket got up and asked Dad where he stood on building a wall along the Canadian border to keep out illegal immigrants. Dad looked him straight in the eye, like he did with all his constituents, then made a bad mistake—he burst out laughing. A wall to keep out Canadians!

Billings, who was a fast learner, immediately jumped up.

"That's an idea worth considering," he said, nodding vigorously. "I know Mr. Lilly Liberal over there thinks otherwise, but we need to start a genuine conversation about this before things get out of hand."

Dad fought back, but feebly, not like he would have even two years before. I tried to help from California. We take the new sales recruits mountain biking in the hills to test their mettle, and, Ian being Ian, he makes sure he beats them all to the top. I caught up with him while he was still panting in victory.

"So Ian? All those Democrats you like to support around the country? I've got another one for you who's in a tough spot."

He pushed his bike helmet back, gave me that look of bemusement he saves for underlings who surprise him.

"No one's ever asked me for just five thousand before," he said when I finished.

"It's to buy an ad on TV. Local station. Just one ad."

Dad didn't accept the money of course—he was happy with his lawn signs. On an impulse, without stopping to examine my motives, I decided to fly east on election day, made all the arrangements, hesitated, then, when that Tuesday finally came, surprised myself by actually getting on the plane. I didn't tell Dad I was coming. I'd rent a car in Boston, drive north in time to be there when the results started coming in.

And that's the way it turned out. Connections went

smoother than they usually do, the weather was tranquil, and I was crossing into New Hampshire just as it grew dark. I got out at a rest area to check my phone for early returns, and it was much colder than it had been in Boston. It made me remember when I was little, and how in winter the skin would tighten on my cheeks, making me sneeze.

Campaign headquarters was the Holiday Inn in Concord. Security guards slouched on a bench outside the ballroom but weren't checking anyone, not at this stage of the night. Things weren't going well. A congresswoman was being re-elected, and a crowd of reporters buzzed around her, but over on the other side of the room was nothing but disappointed state candidates who looked like wallflowers at a dance pretending they didn't mind being wallflowers.

I spotted Peter Lahm the same moment he spotted me. He had come from Germany as a college student, become fascinated by American politics, and had spent his life trying to understand how it all worked. The years had shrunk him, bent him half over, but he straightened up enough to give me a big hug.

"How's Dad doing?" I asked, though I pretty much knew.

"Better than the polls said. Better than I thought."

"Bad?"

"Massacred."

He started in with a long explanation about why, the issues, the tactics, but I hardly listened. To me it was like listening to an analysis of a football game. Here they were, this roomful of politicians, brain dead most of them, still hitting each other, blocking, tackling, too obtuse to realize the important games were being played elsewhere, by free-booters like Ian who didn't give a damn about sports.

When Peter finished, we both turned automatically to try and locate him. It wasn't hard. He was shaking hands good-bye with some of his oldest supporters, and most of them, I noticed, made sure they patted him on the back as he turned away. He didn't slump like the other losers. If it really had been football and people were choosing up sides, he would have been the first one picked, so much strength did he radiate, so much calm self-possession, even at 78. His white hair only added to this. For the first time in his life he was truly handsome.

Someone turned the music up to make things cheerier, so it was a second before I realized Peter was saying something in my ear.

"You two okay now? You and Bob?"

"I came, didn't I?"

"Yeah, you came. That's important, Sue, your coming. I'm sure he appreciates it."

I waited until Dad finished his goodbyes, then went over just as he was putting on his coat, the old lumberjack one that already had patches when I was little. He was surprised, of course, and gave me a smile that was a lot wider than his politician one, but he didn't reach to hug me like Peter had and I didn't reach to hug him.

"Shit happens," I said, pointing to the TV monitor with the numbers. I didn't know what else to say.

He nodded, kept buttoning his parka. "Serves me right, still asking the world for approval at my age. You eat yet? You hungry?"

"I grabbed a sandwich at the airport."

He squinted down at me. For a second, I thought of when I was twelve, handing him my report card.

"You up for something? You want to help me?"

"Help you what?"

"My pickup's outside. Here's the key. Let me go congratulate the congresswoman, and maybe you can go out and get it warmed up for us."

I had lost my immunity to cold, but, even so, it seemed more intense than earlier. It was like the atmosphere of defeat, so heavy in the ballroom, had gone outside and spread. And I wondered—did that damp coppery smell still mean snow? It seemed impossible that just that morning, on the way to the airport, I had asked my neighbor to water my bougainvillea.

Dad wasn't long in coming out. He always drove white trucks, insisted on keeping them immaculate, so, from habit, he walked around the sides swiping away at any blemishes before climbing into the cab. In the overhead light, in the brief second it flashed on, I saw his expression. Never, not even at Mom's funeral, had I seen such pain.

"How's that beautiful little granddaughter of mine?" he asked, reaching for the seatbelt.

He needed to get that out of the way before we left.

"Fine. I had an e-mail from Doug this summer. He said she's excited about starting first grade."

Okay—one baby step toward pretending to be comfortable. He backed out of the parking lot too fast, swerved left on Main Street like the cops were chasing us, but still said nothing about where we were going or why. It was like he assumed I knew, and it would have been dumb of me to ask. We turned onto a quieter street, headed west on a back road that had no lights. Fifteen minutes along this, where the first hills started, we must have crossed into his senate district, and, like we were safe now, he finally slowed down.

"So," he said, taking his hands off the wheel just long enough to spread his fingers apart. "You have to think about sight lines, morning sunshine, readability. You want them out by themselves, not hidden by anyone else's. Don't put them anywhere pretty, because people get mad at you for blocking the view. Soil's important—you want those stakes deep enough they don't blow over. Put them right side for the morning commute, left side for people coming home. Morning's more important. The kind of person I want makes their decision in the morning, not at midnight. Midnight ones are the haters, and they've never had much use for me."

What was he talking about? I still felt slow. But then, abruptly, he swerved to the side of the road, put the flashers on, got out. I had no choice but to get out with him.

Past the shoulder was a narrow strip that had more litter than grass—our shoes crunched down on milk cartons and beer cans. He stopped near a sign, which the next car's headlights, cutting across our legs, made bright and garish as a billboard. *You're My Boss Vote Bob Lilly.*

He looked down at it in a pensive way, like he had never seen such a sign before, never read such a message. But that didn't last long, the pensive part. He reached, grabbed the top, pulled, then, when it came loose, handed it over to me stake and all.

"Uh great. Thank you, Dad. A souvenir."

I heard him laugh. "Well, not exactly."

"What am I supposed to do with it then?"

He nodded in the direction of the truck. "Lay it flat in back. Shove it up against the side so there's room for more."

Across the road was another sign, and without bothering to check for traffic he walked over in those long, purposeful strides of his and took that one, too. Ten seconds later, after I put both where he told me, we started out again. There was a traffic circle up ahead, and we stopped there next, though this time he was careful to pull the truck completely off the road. He had to search a bit—supporters put signs up on their own, he hadn't planted all of them—but then we found three in a row. They were deeper than the others, the ground was starting to freeze, so he really had to tug to get them out.

"That makes five," he said, laying these new ones across my outstretched arms. "Nine hundred and ninety-five left to go."

Did he really mean to do that, collect them all? He had never been a man to do things by half. The next ten miles must have been a Republican enclave . . . he never planted signs here, he explained, because they just got stolen . . . but then he pulled to the side, twisted his head around, backed us up onto a muddy driveway.

"Jason Burt, almost forgot about his. Farmed both sides of the highway, gave it up to developers, though it damn near broke his heart. Old-time Yankee, kind they don't make anymore—never wastes a penny. He saves my signs in his barn, brings them out every two years, even though they're all dirty and faded. I was able to help with Human Services when his wife got sick, gave them a little kick in the pants . . . Well, no need for him to save *this* one."

He yanked out the sign with a grunt, handed it over. The paper part was damp with a cold dust that I was ludicrously slow in recognizing as snow. We had been climbing since Concord, we were well out into the hills, and the temperature was still dropping. When I got back into the cab, seeing me shiver, Dad took his gloves off and handed them over.

"Bog Cambiasso's place is up ahead somewhere, keep your eyes peeled. Bog and Linda. They always go a bit crazy, put out ten or eleven signs, makes it seems like I'm leading a whole parade. He used to be the mortgage man at the bank here, helped out when Mom and I started the summer camp and no one else would take a chance on us. Before his stroke, we used to go grouse hunting every October."

I counted . . . eleven signs, just like he predicted . . . and we had to start a second layer in the back.

"Kipper Johansson," Dad said, a hundred yards up the road. "Always gave me hell, said I was selling out to the corporations, but every year, right on Labor Day, up goes a sign. Old union man. His grandfather fought the scabs down in Manchester, and his father did, too. I'll have to give him a call someday—" He glanced over at me, smiled the quick ironic way I remembered. "Now that I have time."

When we entered a village the signs were clustered closer together, so we were able to collect a dozen or more at one pass. Soon, we had five layers in the back, thanks to us climbing in and stomping down on them, but soon there wasn't room for even one more.

We'll have to quit now, I decided—I surprised myself

by feeling disappointed. But Dad had already figured out a solution. He was pals with all the local road agents, state roads having been one of his legislative priorities, and so we drove to the nearest highway garage, dumped the signs in a big pile near the road salt where he could go back later in the week and get them.

"What happens then?" I asked.

He shrugged. "Burn them. Maybe invite the neighbors over to watch. Serve cider and donuts. Those stakes are kiln-dried pine, they'll burn nice and hot."

Somewhere along the way he began leaning over the steering wheel with more intensity than before, and I wondered if he was having trouble seeing. Cataracts were an issue, and there had been warnings about glaucoma. He remembered where a lot of signs were, but I was better at actually spotting them, and more and more it was me telling him to pull over rather than the other way around.

I used the old trick of staring down at the side of the road, not right toward where the flakes blew thickest. And it wasn't just signs I was looking for. All the years away had made me forget how snow could seem like a scrim, one that you could almost see through and yet not quite, giving you the sense that, if you only stared harder, reached deeper, you could penetrate the whiteness to something that wasn't ordinarily visible, something important.

They were red, white, and blue, his signs—did I mention that? They were made for him by a printing firm up north that had been in business since 1925. Every one was the same size, three feet by four. One I found had LIBBERAL! scrawled next to his name, and another had a swastika.

It was after midnight now. We had collected probably 300 signs, which meant we still had 700 to find by
dawn. By dawn—that was important, though I was slow
in understanding why. He had been defeated, whipped,
humiliated, and the only way he could deal with that was
to have it all end now. Not tomorrow, not next week—now.
On Election Day, Tuesday, the signs represented hope,
even defiance, but when the sun rose Wednesday all they'd
represent was trash.

When Mom died, he had done the same thing with her
clothes, given them away the day after the funeral, carting
off box after box to the thrift store. The relatives had been
shocked at his haste, but not me. We're both so alike in that
respect. When we turn a page we turn it for good.

We were driving back roads now, with potholes and
washboard that forced him to slow down. He had been
born in this part of the county, he had fished it, hiked it,
hunted it, and knew most of the families, or had back in
the days before rich people began putting up castles. Peter
Lahm, in one of his columns, called Dad the only politician
left who still made house calls, and that wasn't much of an
exaggeration.

"Zane Stranahan lives over there," he said, pointing out
the windshield to a vague gray rectangle. "You ever hear me
talk about Zane Stranahan?"

"The one who threw manure on you?"

"That was another Zane Stranahan. Didn't like my
position on the sales tax. And it wasn't manure, it was cow
piss . . . No, this Zane Stranahan is the unluckiest man in
the state, and also probably the gentlest. Had to take care
of his parents when they were sick, never got to go off on

his own like most young men. Married a beauty, Wanita, but she got Lou Gherig's and died. His daughters, both of them, had to be institutionalized, he couldn't care for them alone. That was back in 1982 when the politicians were closing up the hospital, farming people out to the community, and I was able to get them placed somewhere decent. Now they've taken away even that, the miserly sum we devote to mental illness? Can you imagine? Taking funding away from the needy just to be mean? I should have fought harder to stop it."

The Stranahan place was one of those old farmhouses you still come upon back in the hills, with just enough of a roof to keep it from falling in completely. A light shone through an upstairs window, so maybe his friend was still up, but Dad just went over to collect the lawn sign, which stood by itself near a snow-dusted pine.

Once he pulled it out, instead of handing it to me like the others, he stood there shaking his head. I went over and took it from him, realized right away it was different—bigger than his signs, printed on thicker, glossier paper, with a stake made of metal rather than wood. I shined the flashlight down. *Elect Larry Billings*, it read. *Take Back America!*

Dad stared toward the house and the lonely light. "Zane must have moved," he mumbled, but I could see that it hit him hard.

And I need to say that here—how old Dad seemed, from that point of the night on. He'd been awake for over twenty hours straight, which would have wearied a much younger man, let alone one who was pushing 80. I was the one who climbed in the truck to stuff all the signs down now, he just stood there on the side watching. And now, when he got back in the cab, he was shaking in a way the heater couldn't stop.

I suggested we take a break. Rural New England at 2:00 a.m. is not an easy place to find coffee, but there was a small truck stop back near the interstate, and Dad knew a short-cut. The only patrons that late were truckers on their way down from Quebec, but it seemed best to take the drinks back to the pickup, sit there with the heater on, sharing the quiet in a way I don't think would have been possible at the beginning of our drive.

"Yours hot enough?" he asked, after not saying anything for a while.

"Great. Yours?"

"Super."

And that was it as far as conversation went, at least until our coffees were finished and we were about to start back out.

"I don't know how to ask this," I said, which God knows was the truth. "Before, when we first got into the hills and the snow started? I had a feeling, a memory, and it's become stronger the further we've gone, but I still can't grab it, not without help . . . Once when I was little, five or six. I woke up and I wasn't in my bed, I was in the car with you, and we were driving through the night, and there was no explanation, we were just driving. Mom wasn't with us, and I knew without anyone telling me that it was the latest I'd ever been up. It was cold, so it must have been winter. You had that same coat on, it had patches even then, but when you saw I was shivering, you draped it over my shoulders . . . I must have gone to sleep after that. I don't remember anything but waking up in the car and you driving and me shivering and then getting warm and cozy again and going back to sleep."

"I don't remember," Dad said quickly, but that was reflexive, he wanted to do better than that for me, and I could see him trying to decide just how. He sat up straighter, leaned in toward the wheel, so it was like he was steering again, putting into it all his concentration.

The story didn't take long to tell—he never wasted words when he was serious. I was right—I was five when it happened. Mom was at a school board meeting as the faculty representative, so Dad didn't expect her home until late. He made me scrambled eggs for dinner, we read *The Hungry Caterpillar,* then he put me to bed. About nine the phone rang and it was Mom. She wasn't coming home, she said. She had met a man during the summer when he had come to pick up his son at camp, they had become increasingly serious, and it was time to stop pretending and hiding and sneaking. He was going to London on business, his plane left later that night, and she was going with him to start a new life.

"I didn't respond, didn't say anything. I didn't even feel anything, though I'd had no hint of it until that moment. All I could think about was going after her. I woke you up, wrapped you in your puffy jacket because it was so cold, put you on the back seat with your Big Bird pillow, started out heading toward Boston. I didn't have any more plan than that. I thought, well, I'll catch her on the interstate, even cut her off with the car if I have to, reason with her, bring her back with us . . . You woke up once, and I stopped to make sure you were covered, but other than that you slept

through the whole drive . . . I didn't catch her on the interstate. I drove us all the way to Boston, raced out to Logan,
parked in the taxi lane, carried you into the terminal, asked
what gate the London plane was leaving from, ran toward
security intending to force my way through. But then I saw
Mom, sitting alone on a bench near the coffee shop, looking very sad, very small. When she saw me, she smiled and
waved, and I sat down next to her, and she took you from
me, gently chided me for parting your hair the wrong way.
I knew it was going to be okay when she did that, gave me
a hard time about your hair."

He let go the steering wheel now, reached up to the overhead light, switched it on, switched it off, then, with a nodding motion of the hand, lightly touched my arm.

"It was a hard year after that. Hard for a lot of reasons.
We were both so slow in learning who we truly were. But
know what? It was only after that happened that we started
to be happy."

We heard voices then, the truckers coming back out to
their rigs, calling out to each other in French. I waited until
their lights cut across us in the absorbent grains of snow.

"Dad?"

"Right here, Susan."

"I've been going to a fertility preservation clinic. I've
started the procedure. Freezing your eggs? The company
pays for it. I might be happy I did someday. " I wanted to
look at him, see his reaction, but instead I just shrugged.
"Anyway, I started it, and it's no big deal. Ian budgets it
under productivity."

He could always stare at me longer than I could stare at
him. He finally nodded, then jerked his thumb like a hitch-
hiker toward the road.

"Three hundred and seventy-six signs left to go. Feel up to it?"

"Want me to drive?"

"That would be great, Sue. My eyes are tired, so that would be great."

We didn't get 376 signs. We got maybe a hundred more, loaded up the truck two more times, drove another 60 miles. We used up the rest of the night, outlasted the snow, and when we finally stopped it was on a highway overlook in the mountains facing east. In that country, in that month, daybreak looks a lot more like sunset than it does dawn, and Dad must have sensed that even more strongly than I did.

We got out of the truck, walked together toward the railing put there to keep sightseers from falling off, holding hands in the slush so neither of us would slip.

"Gone," he said, staring eastward. He said it loud, like he was testing the echo or trying to be heard all the way down in the statehouse. Even so, it wasn't loud enough for him, so he cupped his hands across his mouth and shouted. "Gone!"

I don't know what he meant by that, though I spent the flight back west trying to guess. Gone? What's gone? Gone for good? Gone forever? *Gone?* Knowing Dad, it's not something small.

# DAY ONE

HE CHOKES THE FIRST EGG, there's so much anger left in his hands. It isn't deliberate—he immediately feels sorry for it, or at least the cold globby mess left in his hands. He cradles it over to the sink, lets it slide into the drain basket, then turns on the faucet to force the glutinous part down where he won't have to see it, the evidence of his complete and utter incompetence.

Egg number two cracks no better. He taps it three times on the edge of the bowl, but that's one tap too many—the shell explodes into the white like shrapnel, and try as he might he can't pick the pieces back out. He is soft on animate things, hard on inanimate, but where on that scale does an egg fall? The third one he pictures as living, sensitive, sentient—its ovoid shape seems ready to smile. Gently now, he tells himself—but violence is violence, and when he breaks the egg open it turns out to be a bloody one that disgusts him.

He doesn't know much about eggs other than eating them. Her cookbooks are arranged on a shelf near the dishwasher, but they are for masters, not for the likes of him. Might as well have sent her to consult his engineering manuals when she wanted to change a lightbulb—these were not books that would explain the basics. Before destroying any more eggs, he carefully examines the pink carton they perch in, wondering if like soup cans or lasagna boxes it will include a recipe.

There's lots to read there. *Hudson Fresh*, it says, and *Keep refrigerated*, and *Fresh Grade A Extra Large* and *Fresh eggs are produced on our own farm in the fresh air of the mountains close to where you live.* There's a cartoon of a mother hen explaining to her chick about what freshness means. Both have antlers perched on their heads and Santa Claus beards crayoned below their beaks, and while this was entirely like her, in keeping with her sense of humor, he marvels at how in the pain of it, the overwhelming suddenness, she had found the capacity to doodle.

*You can't make an omelet without breaking eggs.* He's heard that a thousand times, people were always quoting it while causing others hurt, but it's the only thing like a recipe he knows, his only guidance. She never let him cook in their 38 years together, though they had shared most of life's other tasks. I'm spoiled, he told his friends, but sometimes he wondered if it wasn't a deliberate ploy on her part, increasing his dependence, binding him to her the same way some men wouldn't let their wives take a job.

He tried barbecuing once, back in the lost years. Friends came over, he'd had a drink or two or three, scorched the hamburgers, knocked the grill over, set the lawn on fire.

Now he felt like he had been yanked out of his seat on a plane, told that he's now the pilot. He interlocks his fingers, flexes them outwards—he windmills his arms around and takes a deep breath—but when he reaches for a new egg his arm hits the mixing bowl, and, avoiding the desperate belly he shoves at it, shatters apart on the floor.

"Shit!" he yells. With no one in the house to hear, the sound goes nowhere.

The bowl's shards are like thicker, sharper eggshells—he kicks them under the counter, then takes her nesting bowls down from the top of the refrigerator. They're metal, not porcelain, and in the deepest is a package of beef she had left there to defrost before it all happened. It smells like sugared gasoline—he adds it to the trash with the murdered eggs and slaps on the lid.

Time to change tactics. He ignores the eggs for the time being, turns his attention to the frying pan. It's a heavy one, big enough for cowboys to use over a campfire, but he wants to make sure he has ample room. When he puts it on the back burner its bottom overlaps onto the front one, so he turns both to their highest setting. He's reasonably sure she always added something to the pan before dropping in the eggs, but was it butter, olive oil, lard? Butter, he guesses. He breaks off half a stick, thinks about it, drops in the other half, goes off to the bathroom to shave.

He's finished, he's rinsing his face, when with remarkable clarity, as if she were speaking the words directly into his ear, he remembers something his mother always said when he was little, his mother who never used aphorisms, or at least just this one. *Never walk away from butter.* It impressed him tremendously—that this was the only rule of life she ever thought worth expressing—and now here he had violated that rule on his very first try. He hurries back to the kitchen, but too late—from the frying pan arises a greasy brown steam, and what butter is left is the color and consistency of licorice.

He grabs the handle, burns himself, curses, throws it in the sink, turns on the cold. A blister immediately rises on the webbing of his thumb, but he can't let it bother him, not now. He goes into the pantry to search for another frying pan, something smaller and more manageable, finds one on the lowest shelf sitting atop the ring stains left by his bottles back in the days when bottles, the contents of bottles, mattered to him greatly. He rubs the tip of his finger around the biggest ring, brings it to his lips—but the stains are from sixteen years ago, and no taste remains.

From the six eggs remaining he plucks out the one that looks hardiest, most willing. He tried to be gentle before, but now he tries even harder. He thinks of the first time he ever touched her, the joy and trepidation with which his hand found hers on the steps of the Worcester Public Library, main division, in 1972. That's the way to do it, he tells himself—lightly, casually, the tenderness flowing down in baby-step surges—but he can't hold the memory quite long enough, so what he's drawing upon isn't gentleness, but the exact opposite: all the disasters and fuck-ups his hands have been involved in during their 71 years of operation. The egg, being no match for these, implodes in his palms.

The next egg is the smallest, the pinkest pale—when he picks it up, it seems to blush. I'll treat you like a baby, he decides, but what on earth does he know about babies? They were ready for one when they were younger, had in a fit of optimism added on a room big enough for twins, then made it into a TV room when no twins came. In the health class she taught at school, in the section on parenting, she paired a boy with a girl, gave them an egg to take care of so they could learn about responsibility. In the first years, the eggs were always returned safely at the end of the month; in her last years, the eggs usually got smashed within twenty-four hours.

So. Baby egg—egg with a talcum-colored bottom. His hands seemed to get the message, find just the right amount of tenderness, so the shell, once he taps it, separates more than cracks. From the cup-shaped bottom he pours out the yolk, then takes the last egg and does similar. They look good against the silver of the mixing bowl—the yolks round and golden as planets. He knows he's supposed to stir them, but when he takes a spoon, starts swirling, the planets revolve around each other without losing their shapes, and it's only when he tries stirring with a fork that mixing occurs—the yellow spreads apart like a map of China or Brazil.

Pepper is next—he likes things spicy—but when he turns the shaker over, the top falls off, creating an avalanche of black. He takes the spoon, scoops as much from the surface as he can, then goes to the refrigerator for milk. Christmas cards from friends who haven't heard yet are held there beneath magnets—the first sympathy cards, too. He stares at them, decides for the hundredth time to save reading them for after, though he has no idea when after will come.

The milk carton is nearly impossible to open. The top gets all sticky and mashed, so he takes a paring knife and gives it a tracheotomy, cutting an opening in its throat. Big mistake. When he brings it to the bowl, tilts it over, half the contents gush out, flooding China is a sea of white.

"Fuck!" he says. Again, with no one listening, it's hardly worth bothering.

There are no more eggs. He searches the cabinet, finds, not the colander he's looking for, but his old collection of shot glasses, one from every state he had ever taken a drink in, back in the days he'd tried pouring the country down his throat. He's surprised that she had saved them, all 43. He reaches for the nearest—Arizona, with a cactus embossed on the glass—puts it on the counter for what purpose he's not sure.

He goes through two more cabinets before finding the colander. He sets it across the sink, pours the bowl into it, hoping the milk will separate from the eggs and he can start over. And while some of the milk does run out, the rest seems glued to the yolks in a pus-like bonding that sloshes over the grates without separating. He flips the colander over, turns on the tap to flush it all away.

He goes back to the refrigerator, pushes everything aside, finds two eggs in a little dish, brings them back out, taps them against the counter edge, but all they do is bounce. Hardboiled—she must have been making egg salad—and he's reasonably certain that in making an omelet hardboiled is useless.

Nine o'clock now—he always ate breakfast at eight. He doesn't feel hunger, but emptiness and loss, which are hardly the same thing. On the counter near her African violets is the box of Cheerios she bought him before leaving for the hospital, but he doesn't want to surrender, not yet.

He remembers his stepfather clomping downstairs for

breakfast when he was little, dressed in a robe thick as a monk's. "Time to break fast!" he would say, slapping his stomach, explaining, like the enthusiast he was, how fasting was no bad thing, allowing you visions and insights that wouldn't come when you were sated. Visions and insights, though, are the very last thing he's interested in, not under these circumstances, and he knows he'd better eat soon.

Decision time. He goes to the window, gauges the sky. The sun, what he can see of it, is surrounded by the kind of halo that presages snow, so if he's going to do it, he'd better do it now. He takes his overcoat from the closet, goes out to the car, remembers his gloves, goes back in for them, goes out, remembers change for parking, goes in, then stands stock still in the entryway with his eyes shut, trying to let this wild imbalance slowly settle. It does, finally. With a defiant little punching motion he manages to leave the house.

It's cold enough he has to scrape the windshield. Halfway out the driveway the dashboard starts beeping, and he hears, as clearly as if spoke out loud, her gentle admonition.

"Put on your seatbelt, Peter."

God will protect me, he always shot back. But you don't believe in God, she answered. True, he admitted—and with that settled, always put on his belt.

But not today. Today, in a sudden rush of defiance, he leaves it off. Whatever force rules the world can watch over him for a change. He never asked much of it—damn little in fact. By the time he gets to the corner the beeping stops and he no longer hears her voice.

It's snowing in town. The Big Z parking lot is crowded with people getting ready for Christmas, and he has to circle before finding a spot—then, once he does, backs right out again. He doesn't feel up to fighting the mob just for eggs, even less capable of talking to any of her yoga pals or book club buddies who might be shopping. Across Main is a convenience store called Bumby's. He parks near the gas pumps, leaves the  motor running, goes in to the cooler, takes out a dozen eggs, thinks about it, takes out another dozen, then a third.

"Ain't Easter," grunts the man at the register. He reaches up and tugs at his Santa hat to drive the point home.

"True," Peter mumbled, then "You can't make an omelet without breaking eggs."

The man refuses to be topped. "Sure you can," he says—but then another customer drops matching six-packs on the counter, and if the man has a secret, he's too busy to explain.

Peter arranges the egg cartons end to end across the back seat, pads his scarf over them so they won't roll off. He's in his errand mode, but he can't really think of any—and then suddenly he does. A hundred yards down the highway, he puts the blinker on, turns left into another huge lot.

The Miss Florence Diner is the only place in town not run by chains. Though it's well past breakfast time, there's a line waiting to get in. People off from work, families, teenagers, all of them swatting at the snow or leaning back their mouths to catch the flakes.

The line moves at a good clip. A waitress comes out hugging her bosom in the cold. "How many?" she asks. "Two," he says automatically, then is too embarrassed to call her back. When she comes out again, she's holding two menus. "I'm sorry," he says. "I mean one."

"No problem, big guy," she says, in a great waitress voice. She goes down the line. "Two? Two? Two?"

Everyone is two—but then she comes back again, takes his arm. "One?"

"One," he says.

She leads him to the counter, sits him down between a priest fat enough to take up two stools and a cop so skinny three of him could sit on one. But he's lucky—he's directly opposite the grill, which is what he hoped for. The short-order chef is a young girl, beautiful if not for her tattoos, and she has a flirty way of peering up at the orders pinned on the ventilator hood. Egg cartons are lined up where she can easily reach them, and the tops have been ripped back so she can pluck them out fast.

It's only a matter of time before someone orders an omelet—or is it? Miss Florence is famous for pancakes, and that's what everyone is ordering—doughy circles punctuated by sausage take up most of the grill. Someone finally orders eggs, but sunny side up, and while she handles these expertly, there aren't any lessons he can learn from and take home.

His friend the waitress, noticing he hasn't been served, comes over with her pad.

"Ya' have?"

Cheese omelet, is what he wants to say. Cheese omelet so I can see for myself how your chef makes one. But then, of course, he will have to eat it, or be tempted to eat it, and end up proving nothing.

"Coffee," he says. "Regular, thanks."

He nurses it for as long as possible, but no one orders an omelet, the lunch crowd starts coming in, and by the time he leaves it's all hamburgers on the grill or fancy looking paninis.

It's snowing harder now—the flakes are the small kind that mean business—but it's too soon to return to the house. He needs another stop, it hardly matters where. His numbness is starting to wear off around the edges, melting like the snow on his windshield, so he'll soon have to look at things plain. When he comes to the next plaza, the car turns in by itself, volition has nothing to do with it, or that's what he tells himself. "Like a horse to the barn," he mumbles—the Liquor Barn, a red shed of a place that hasn't changed in the sixteen years since he'd last gone in.

It smells like a barn, that's the funny thing, as if pigs were stabled there, not bourbon. The linoleum looks like turf splattered with cow pies, and boxes are piled in the corner like brown bales of hay. Only the bottles add color—many of them have Christmas ribbons around their throats—and it makes them look even more appealing than they would in a store that's less filthy.

A man his age guards the cash register. He's no farmer— he looks like someone who would lead cows to slaughter— and his face is smeared in liver spots. He puts the newspaper down, gets up lethargically, then, seeing him, squints with sudden interest.

"Long time no see," he says with a leer.

Peter doesn't remember him—the last time he came in he wasn't memorizing faces—but it's clear the man remembers him.

"Usual?" he asks.

Just looking, Peter almost says, then realizes that's ridiculous. "Sure," he says. He waits at the counter, curious as to what the man will bring back.

Jack Daniels, and not a small one. The man sets it down on the counter, gives it a twirl as if showing off its figure.

"Probably won't want this gift-wrapped," he says, then, with another leer, "Drink responsibly, pal. See you next time."

Peter looks back through the window when he leaves—the man is staring after him with a phone to his ear, as if warning the police.

He drives straight home. The driveway is slippery with snow, and while normally he would skate across this without thinking, he takes mincing old-man steps, afraid he will fall. It's the eggs, he tells himself—I can't afford to drop them.

The house, for all its emptiness, offers warmth. He puts the eggs down on the kitchen table, goes to the bathroom to pee, comes back and takes them out from their cartons, lining them up across the counter like the short-order chef at the diner. They wobble in their oval way, as if they're nervous, sensing their fate, but then that quiets and they rest at ease like soldiers after a parade. He goes for the bourbon bottle, sets it on the far right of the line where it can act as their sergeant.

Standing near the stove, her stove, feels even odder than it had in the morning—he expects at any moment to hear her not-so-gentle remonstrance. Sundays were omelet days, and he would often sneak up while she was cooking, put his hands on her waist, wait until her shoulder rose, her neck dipped, and then kiss her on the cool, delicious hollow beneath her curls. He loved these moments—and yet now he wished that, at least once anyway, he had peeked over her shoulder to see how she did it.

But he's confident now, calmer—or at least tells himself he is. After he put his career back together, in his last project before retiring, he had worked on stress calculations for the new buildings at Ground Zero, and what is making an omelet compared to that?

And it goes well, cracking the eggs. They separate nicely, behave themselves in the bowl, and this time he mixes in only a cup of milk, not the half quart he spilled earlier. He searches the refrigerator for cheese, finds an unwrapped chunk of cheddar and a small crock of spread. He assumes the spread is the one to use, since it's already halfway to melting, but is he supposed to add it now or toward the finish? He scoops some in a spoon, plops it in the middle of the bowl, stirs hard clockwise, then even harder counter clockwise.

Frying pan next—a small one not much wider than the omelet he pictures making. Last time he'd put the burner too high, so now he turns the dial to the lowest setting. He adds in the half stick of butter left from earlier, waits five minutes before it starts melting, then dumps the bowl's contents in the pan's middle.

He's reasonably sure it's supposed to sizzle, the slurry liquid against the hot pan, but it barely even hums. He stares down at it—its limpidity reminds him of tidal pools on the Maine coast where they vacationed. Nothing much seems to happen other than a bubble now and then. He knows he must be patient, give it time. He goes to the bedroom, drags the vacuum out from under the bed, readies it for later, then, on the way back to the kitchen, remembering how she did it, kicks a rug against the door to keep out drafts.

Even then he doesn't approach the stove right away. He gets out a plate, a fork and napkin, arranges them on the table with a glass of orange juice he pours from the fridge. Then and only then does he check what's happening.

The eggs bubble like a pot of boiling white paste, but still haven't congealed—they're sloshed sideways in the pan as if trying to escape over the rim. He understands immediately what's wrong—the stove is off level. He yanks the frying pan from the burner, pours the contents in the trash, pulls and shoves until the unit comes away from the wall.

There are petrified crumbs behind it, blackened bits of celery, mouse droppings, toothpicks. He cleans these up as best he can, appraises things, goes to the garage for some lumber scraps, comes back, stiffly kneels, places shims under the metal legs on the left so they match the metal legs on the right—pushes the stove back to the wall and tries again.

This time he puts the heat on medium, adds only a quarter cup of milk, two tablespoons of butter, and is rewarded by hearing the mixture sizzle when it hits the pan. The bubbles look better, too—not small and fizzy like they were last time, but blisters thick as lava.

He rummages through three drawers before finding a spatula, though it seems too narrow to flip anything wider than mushrooms. In the pan, the eggs have stiffened to the point where they look foldable. Is this the moment to add cheese? The crock stuff has disappeared into the yellow, so it obviously needs another shot. He breaks off a big wedge of cheddar, drops it in the middle, stares down waiting for something to happen. The bottom melts, but the top juts out like the tip of an iceberg. He can't wait much longer—already, the bottom of the eggs are starting to blacken—so he dives in with the spatula, pressing down to flatten it against the pan's bottom, then twisting.

Part of the mixture lifts, but the other part breaks off, so he's left with two separate egg masses, both of which are now burnt. He throws it all in the trash, wipes the pan out with paper towels, reaches for two new eggs, starts over. He adds flour to the mix this time, thinking it might stiffen things, make it easier to turn. It doesn't—the next eggs represent a soggy step backwards—so he pours them in the trash and starts over.

It's not breakfast he's making anymore—it's well past lunchtime. Already, with the days being so short, the kitchen is dark enough he has to put on the lights. Somewhere in the next three attempts he gets the milk right and the butter right and the heat right, but he's still having trouble with the flipping and the cheese. He makes himself coffee, sits at the table sipping it while he stares at the remaining eggs. Twenty-two left before the bourbon bottle. The neighbors have already turned on their Christmas lights, and enough comes through the window that the eggs look dusted in blue and green.

The bourbon bottle doesn't look dusted, it looks bejeweled, as if the green Christmas light, hitting it, has turned the glass into emerald. He knows that trick, remembers it from the lost years—how liquor appropriates whatever is brightest in a room, whatever is happiest, most joyous, so, if you want that happiness, there's only one thing to grab. And sadness—it works just as well with sadness, or why else would the bottle look so lonely now, bright as it is? It needs holding. It needs comforting. It needs someone to take its cap off so it can sigh.

He remembers a rule he had always ignored: *never drink on an empty stomach*. The eggs, when he stares at them, seem sitting straighter now, like students eager to be called on. So goddamn young looking—so goddamn prim. The heavy, defeated feeling in his shoulders spreads down his arms, but his fingers still feel stubborn, enough so he gets up from the table and goes back over to the stove.

Tenderness hasn't worked. Patience hasn't worked. He decides to give anger another chance, starts cracking eggs like each and every one of them has personally affronted him. The first shatters so explosively the yolk stains his pants, the next one goes into the bowl but gets spilled when he reaches for the milk, the third and fourth make it into the frying pan but when he adds Tabasco it looks all bloody and plasma-like, so he gags. The burner goes cold, and when he pulls it out, pushes it back in again, it shorts in a flash that sets the smoke detectors to screaming. He starts over using the smaller burner—fails, starts over, fails, starts over, working his way down the dwindling row of eggs. He has one omelet that looks promising, readies the spatula under it, leaves for a moment when he hears a siren race by, comes back to find the spatula melted, the eggs all gangrenous and foul. He shakes oregano across the next one, too much of it, which creates a bitter medicinal smell. He tries corn starch to thicken it, baking powder to make it rise, but that's like forcing chemo drugs down a patient who only asks to die. He starts over, fails, starts over, fails . . . and then suddenly he can't do it any longer, the heaviness in his arms runs down to his fingertips where he can't hold it back.

He grabs the frying pan by the handle, flings it as hard as he can toward the sympathy cards on the refrigerator. The pan hits them edge on, caroms back toward his knees, dumping its contents on the floor. He kicks at the mess, stomps on it, rubbing his slippers across the grease. He'd rub his nose in it, if he wasn't so arthritic. Pee on it. Shit on it. Puke on it. Drown it in frustration and defeat.

He stumbles into the darkened living room, gropes with his legs until they find the couch, lets himself collapse on the cushions like he'd drunk the bourbon after all. A second after his head hits the pillows he's unconscious, or as good as. He dreams of basketball, of being in high school again and sinking all his shots—of youth and victory, when nothing could stop him.

It doesn't last long, the dream. He can't have slept more than twenty minutes. He's aware of sounds outside—a plow driving by, a delivery truck shifting gears, and then something that for one horrible second he thinks must be carolers come to serenade him, then realizes is merely the wind.

He listens, but doesn't open his eyes, not for a long time. Sleeping it off, he tells himself, like in the bad days when that's all he ever did, sleep life off. Back then, waking on this very couch, fighting back through the stupor, self-pity, and guilt, he always expected not to find her there once his eyes opened—not see her in the chair across from him, not see her in the kitchen, not find her in the house. She'd had it, thrown in the towel, lost patience, given up caring, checked out—and who could blame her? But she had always been there, looking over at him with the same mix of tenderness, concern, and hurt.

Now? He expects to see her, opens his eyes in absolute certainty she'll be there, sees no one. "I'm sorry, Peggy," he says to the darkness around her chair. He's about to say more, has the words all formed, but there's something preventing him, and he has to force himself to a sitting position, shake his head a few times, bite at the bad taste, before understanding what it is.

Hunger. There's no mistaking it, though he's never been hungry like that before. The feeling isn't centered in his stomach—all his organs and joints seem to share in it equally, with a yearning kind of insistence that makes him weak. Hollowness doesn't begin to describe it—it's not the lack of something, but a positive, pounding force that makes any other emotion impossible to sustain. It's as if, having nothing else to eat, his insides have started munching on loss and sorrow, digesting them into something much simpler, more basic.

He goes to the kitchen, takes a broom and dust pan, wets some paper towels, gets busy cleaning up. Finishing, he takes off his clothes, throws them in the direction of the basement, changes into the track suit he wears when working out. There's a light in the stove's hood, and once he turns it on everything stands out in bolder detail. Under it, his hands look steadier, younger, more supple—in them he feels, not anger anymore, but sureness, the rough beginnings of competency.

There are four eggs left. He takes two of them, breaks them into the newly cleaned bowl, goes for milk, remembers it's all gone, thinks for a moment, makes his decision.

He finds the Arizona shot glass, wets the bottom with a smoky trickle of Jack Daniels, takes the bottle, sniffs, grimaces, dumps the rest of its contents down the sink. He beats the eggs, adds in salt, shakes in pepper, pours in the remaining shot of booze. He's no chemist, but it seems to bind the mixture together in a way the milk hadn't, so it looks reasonably omelet-like even before he adds it to the pan.

He doesn't take his eyes off it while it cooks, not for a second. When the edges begin to bubble, he tilts the pan to the side so the liquid on top spreads to the rim. After so many failures, he's learned when to add the cheese—just before turning over the edge—and he cuts off thin slices, not big chunks. He turns it perfectly, right half over left half, and the underside turns out to be a rich tan color, like the eggs have been sunbathing.

It looks edible—a little on the flat side, but definitely edible. It could pass muster at the diner. A Frenchman wouldn't sneer at it. Any beginner would be satisfied. He takes it to the trash and dumps it in.

Two eggs left. *Try us!* They could be shouting, or *Our turn!* Before, he had nothing to draw upon but ignorance, but now he has experience behind him, and if he's learned nothing else in life it's how to use experience. He adds a tablespoon of water to the mixture to replace the bourbon. He turns the heat a fraction higher, waits a bit longer to turn over the edge, shaves his cheese slices even thinner. When he does finally turn it, the eggs puff up perfectly, so it's an omelet that's domed.

While it was cooking, he pushed down the toast—even in his bad days, he'd always been a decent man with toast—and now he goes to the refrigerator for his favorite Swiss jam. He slides the omelet onto a plate, sets it down on the table between the silverware and a red Christmas napkin.

Too pretty to eat, he decides—it's the yellow of sunflowers, freckled with brown—and then, while still admiring it, he takes his first bite. There's a flakiness, a creamy egg taste, a pleasant saltiness—and then the butter kicks in, with the rich surprise of the melted cheese. Even before he swallows, his hunger is gone, or at least the insistent part. He eats slowly, making a little sandwich out of the last bite, then pushes back the plate as a sated man would after Christmas dinner. He's tasted better omelets in his day, but he's tasted much worse. Very distinctly, as if she's sitting across from him, he remembers what she said in their last moments together when the nurse left the room: "You can't even cook an egg!"

It was impossible to describe how much emotion she put into this. A woman bailing out of a marriage might say those words, dooming her husband to misery. An abused woman might say those words, after enduring so much—sarcastically, as a taunt. A dying woman might say those words—tenderly, tremulously, worried what would become of him, fearing more than anything leaving him behind. There had been traces of all three in her tone, she closed her eyes on the hard truth of it, and he could do nothing to soften it but take her hand, bring his mouth down to her ear, whisper "I'll learn."

# ASSASSINS

BANK STREET BAR & GRILL IS ON BANK STREET, a bank shot across from the bank, which, being near the river, sits on a bank. Mondays at noon you'll find me sitting at our usual table dressed in a banker's grey suit. In fact, you can bank on it, since I'm a banker. And so I start my story with my bankrupt puns, the better to convince you I'm not as biased in this class warfare business as you might think. I'm a student of war, not a soldier on the front lines, and the Bank Street Grill is hardly the trenches.

We're called the Linebackers, the four of us who lunch there, though only Zumbado played in college. He's a developer, and for all his size is the gentlest man I know, and always orders the quiche. Father Robinette is our priest, and he's even thicker and stronger than Zumbo—we'd play him at tackle if we were actually a team. Tommy Rosen was our congressman in Washington for six terms and retired poorer than when he went in. He orders the tuna plate, asks Carly for a container to bring home leftovers.

We take our responsibility to town very seriously, so the talk always turns to various civic projects we're supporting.

A softball field so the girls can play at night. Expanding our sewer system to reach the mall planned south of downtown. Changing the composition of the zoning board. Hiring more police. We're all involved, either as chair or co-chair, and by the time we've finished dessert we usually have solutions to whatever problems are causing delays.

The Monday on which this happened was the first day of spring. The weather was warm enough that tables had been opened out on the terrace. Sitting there under the specials blackboard, their backs against the ferns, were three seniors from high school: Rod Roberts, Jamie Thomas, Carleton Sachs. They ate there often—the high school cafeteria they had long since outgrown—but I could tell from the relaxed way they lounged in their chairs, the knowing little jokes they exchanged with their waitress, the cigar-like way they flourished their French fries, that they were celebrating good news.

College acceptances? They're the best athletes in town, the smartest students, the ones from the best families, so there was nothing particularly surprising about this, other than the fact they had even been required to go through the application process at all.

Father Rob was doing the math on our bill—I had twisted around to pull my wallet out—when I noticed a motion out the window, something just lumpy and grotesque enough that it caught my attention. Three girls walking abreast down the sidewalk pushing a baby carriage, a wobbly black one that looked stolen from a thrift store. Teenagers—the oldest couldn't have been eighteen. An unwed mother with her pals, one heavier than the next, tattoos around their necks like black and blue collars, victimhood written across their faces in what space their overall sadness left blank.

No one noticed them but me—these were not the kind of girls anyone bothers noticing. They stopped by the Grill's entrance, squinted in at the glass-enclosed menu there. The girl actually pushing the baby carriage, the one who looked fractionally smarter, thinner, and more energetic than her friends, reached under its hood, plumped up the blankets just so, then, with a grimly determined expression, signaled the other two to hold the door open, and pushed the carriage inside.

Bill Bannon, the owner, immediately went over to toss them out. He was a gentleman about this—I could hear him explaining there simply weren't any tables available—but the girl pushing the carriage ignored him. She glanced around the dining room, but it was only when she spotted Rod, Carleton, and Jamie out on the terrace that her intentions became clear.

By now, everyone noticed them—people sniggered and pointed. The other two girls, more bovine, backed up toward the ladies room like they knew they had done something wrong. There were blacks at Bank Street that afternoon, Latinos, the handicapped, even gays, but all of them are part of town now, no one hassles them if they can afford to eat there. But these girls? Gatecrashers—and I could sense Bill's embarrassment as he tried figuring out how to eject them without causing a scene.

The only ones who didn't notice this were the three high school boys eating their scampi. The girl with the carriage wedged it crossways between the wall of the grill and the glass of the terrace so no one could get by. She yanked the hood back on her sweatshirt, shook out her curly, brilliantly shiny red hair. She stooped over the carriage, reached down into the blankets, tenderly lifted out her baby—only it wasn't a baby, but what looked to be a Thompson submachine gun, the kind Dillinger might have used back in the Twenties, or Elliott Ness of the FBIU. Immediately, it became the dominant fact in that room—it gathered all the glitter from the silverware, glasses, and plates onto the ebony of its barrel, so once you saw it, it was impossible to turn away.

She brought it down to her hip, took a giant step out onto the terrace where the high school boys were eating. Only now did they notice her—their look of indifference blinked into surprise, then outrage, then fear. Crouching, she sprayed them in two long bursts, Rod to Carleton to Jamie, then back again, Jamie, Carleton, Rod, aiming for their chests where she couldn't miss.

Rod tried ducking, hit his chin on the chair, fell onto the floor taking the tablecloth with him so everything crashed. Carleton clutched his water glass, seemed ready to hurl it, but another burst splattered across his face, forcing him to let go. Jamie ran his hands down his polo shirt, as if he couldn't believe what he was feeling, the pool of wetness that hadn't been there a second before.

The three of them never lost their look of outrage, even as they stoically accepted their fate. Even Carleton, the most egotistical of the three, had the good grace to collapse motionless onto the tiles of the shrimp-littered floor.

Once they were eliminated, the shooter lost all interest in them—she didn't even allow herself a triumphant sneer. Instead, she twirled the gun around with her wrist like a baton, then walked decisively toward the ladies room, against the door of which cowered her two friends, still aghast at being in such an expensive restaurant, never mind what they had just witnessed. They smiled at her, a little uneasily—they seemed to be begging her in what little time they had left.

She put the Thompson to her hip, then hosed them left to right, aiming straight into the v's of their over-tight jeans. The boys had gone down silently, but these were screamers—from the shock of her turning on them more than any pain. They went down like sacks of flour, ruptured sacks, eviscerated ones that squealed.

The entire restaurant was in an uproar now, but the girl, the perpetrator, wasn't finished. She put the gun to her lips, blew softly on the creamy froth dampening its tip, then folded herself over to yank off her sweatshirt. She had on a yellow tank top underneath, a very tight tank top, and what was underneath the tank top immediately replaced the gun as the most dominant two facts in the room.

*Take that!* she yelled—or did I just imagine that? She shoved the gun back into the baby carriage, yanked it backwards to disentangle the wheels from Carleton's loafers, then, on her way out the door, reached across the table, grabbed the leftover shrimp, swallowed it down in one savage gulp.

I watched out the window as she disappeared down the sidewalk into the blankness she had emerged from. The triumph was already gone now, replaced by the most intensely private expression I'd ever seen on a human face.

Do you play Assassins in your town? If you do, it's probably not with our intensity. It's been a tradition here, a rite of passage, ever since the 1960's, just when so many other traditions are dying off. Some bleeding hearts tried stopping it after the Columbine shootings, and then again after Sandy Hook, but we're closing in on the 50th anniversary now and it's more popular than ever. Girls were allowed to participate starting in 1985, and that's done a lot to revitalize things, since so many of them are naturally good at it.

Rules? Three-person teams are formed in high school starting in January, but shooting season is only between March 1 and April 15. No assassinating is allowed on school grounds or at church. Other than that, anything goes.

Or almost anything. While it's perfectly okay to shoot your own teammates, hardly anyone ever does, and the girl turning on her friends in the restaurant was virtually unprecedented. Ambushing people in health clubs or gyms is frowned upon—no explicit stricture yet, but you can sense it coming. And, as in any contest, there are unwritten rules about who can take part. Athletes, honor students, class presidents and vice-presidents, the kids from the best families—they always form the core of our top-tier teams. Most years, no one bothers participating except them, so that was another astonishing thing about the Bank Street massacre—that a girl like that had even dared.

Winners can do very well in town—in fact, it's hard to succeed here unless you *have* done well. Win and your future is golden. Come in second and prospects are still bright. Lower than third, it gets harder, and we've found, over the years, that most of the losers leave town after high school and never come back.

Assassins gives us cohesion, ritual, purpose. Other towns

either hide their competitiveness or shove it off on sports, while here it's out in the open, it doesn't fester. We're notoriously bad at sports—our best athletes get wrapped up in shooting, getting an adrenaline rush that playing football or basketball can't match. Even our little kids catch the fever. In spring, you'll seem them playing outside on their lawns with their junior squirt guns, blasting away at each other, emulating their heroes, the big kids in high school. Too early, some will say. But what other town in America still has kids that play outside on their lawns?

The downside of all this is that people can become outraged very easily if someone bends the rules. When I got back from the restaurant that afternoon, I hid myself in my office, not wanting to be part of the angry discussions going on by the teller windows and in the lobby. About 3:00, I buzzed Cindy, asked her to get me a list of all the seniors at the high school. Cindy being Cindy, it was on my desk five minutes later.

I ran my finger down the column, tapping the names I didn't recognize. I found her in the first column on the second page—my finger knew the moment it touched the name that I had the right one. Crystal Mack. I nodded, smile, looked down at it again. I felt like I knew what I was dealing with now. Crystal Mack. Of course. She could have no other name.

I poured myself a bourbon when I got home, collapsed on the sofa with the remote. Since Jennifer left, I can do things like that—stretch out with a drink, not worry about it spilling. I may have dozed for a while, woke to someone hammering on the door.

"Dad?' I heard a faint voice call. "Let me in Dad, let me in quick."

Roland, through the peephole, looked scared, pissed, and excited all at once. He's a husky kid, much stronger than I was at that age, and you wouldn't think anything could scare him.

"A close one," he said, when I unlocked the door. He didn't elaborate.

I poured him a drink—he's got to learn sometime—and made room for him on the couch. To say our relationship is troubled is to say it's like 99% of the other father-son relationships in town. Roland has virtues, but completely lacks the one I value most—ambition. He has none. Zero. Zilch.

But maybe I'm being too harsh on him. The truth is, he's shown signs of toughening the last few months, and I think not having his mother hovering over him all the time has contributed. He had been recruited by one of the better hit squads—Trevor Limbaugh was on it, whose dad runs the medical center—and he'd put his heart and soul into his assassinations, with five kills to his credit a month before deadline. His grades are awful, he'd gotten nothing but rejections from colleges so far, and it was finally dawning on him that shooting his way to the top was his only option.

He was sweating after his exertions. He kept dipping his fingers into the whiskey, wiping them across his forehead.

"Can you believe what happened?" he said, fury rouging up his cheeks. "The cheating slut! It's outrageous, she should be banned. Why is she even allowed, a person like her? She's breaking every rule in the book."

I took a sip from my glass. "You mean Crystal?"

He seemed surprised that I knew her name.

"Of course Crystal. She's a fucking cheat."

"I was sitting in Bank Street when it happened. Sure, it was a surprise, it caught everyone off guard. But that's the point, right? I didn't see anything that looked like cheating."

"That's not what I'm talking about. After that. She went to the mall to that Morningside Spa place. Terri Murdoch, Heather Goldman, and Megan Bannon were there working out. They were sweaty, they were rehyrdrating themselves by the cooler, when they saw this janitor person pushing what looked to be a mop. They didn't think anything of it— they were talking about this ambush they were planning for tonight—when the janitor lady jumped up and hosed them across their sports bras, just absolutely slaughtered them. Crystal Mack. She had a purple crayon with her and she stepped over them and wrote her name on the wall in big letters like a billboard."

I'm afraid I made a mistake now. I smiled.

"It's not funny. Heather ran into the toilet, and Crystal squirted three more shots into her, though Heather was down on her knees begging for mercy."

Another mistake. I laughed out loud.

He sucked his breath in, ready to annihilate me, which I almost welcomed—anything was better than his usual passivity. But something stopped him. The whisk of shrubbery against the house, a soft crunch of gravel. Something his young ears heard better than mine. He jumped up, hunched himself over, slunk to the door to peer outside.

"Why didn't you have the bushes trimmed? You know they like bushes."

"She's shot enough today."

"It's not her I'm worried about. Crystal? She'd never get past the gatehouse. It's Billy Alito and his team. It would be just like them to bribe the guards. They've got more assets than anyone. Billy's dad bought him this new pump-action, had it flown in from Switzerland. Are the windows closed?"

It was a while before he calmed down. Sitting with his back to the door made him nervous, so I traded places with him on the couch.

"Tell me more about this Crystal girl."

"She's pathetic."

"That's not what I mean."

"She wears camouflage. She goes around with a Trump button. Her hair's the color of deer blood."

"Where does she live?"

"Her father's in prison. Her mother cleans people's houses. She made honor roll last term. She must have cheated."

"Anything else?"

"She's fat. You've seen her. Fat. Obese. Gross."

"Because she has curves? Why do boys your age feel threatened by girls who aren't anorexic?"

"She's been lucky so far. I give her two more days, then—" He slit his hand across his throat.

"She's going around disguised as the people no one sees. A teenage mom. A woman scrubbing floors. It's tactically brilliant. I admire her."

"Admire her? She shouldn't be allowed to participate, Dad. She's from another planet, don't you get that? She's—" He groped with his fist for the right word. "Trailer trash. She's trailer trash, only lower."

My first impulse was to take my drink and throw it into his smug, spoiled, entitled face. I walked over to the door as he had, stood staring out into the black and blue darkness beneath our trees. The limbs looked like plastic soldiers, in that kind of light. Dozens of plastic soldiers crawling on their bellies toward the house, their outstretched arms tapering to fingers as sharp as stilettos.

I turned around. "What kind of trailer?"

"What?"

"There are lots of trailers, so I'm asking you what kind."

"That she lives in? How would I know?"

"There are the ones people use for camping, like Airstreams. Ones they park all summer by lakes, for instance Caravans. Then you have your basic house trailer, including your Pike Industries or your Fuller. I'd like to know which kind you mean."

He bit the top of his glass. "Trailers from hell."

"The one I lived in when I was your age was called a Vulcan. I used to really like that name, it was the only thing I did like. Everything reeked of sewage, the floors sagged no matter where on them you walked, and there were more cracks in the wall than wall itself. But in my room . . . sorry, my closet . . . I could see stamped on the aluminum the words 'Vulcan Manufacturing.' I took great comfort from that. We may have been trailer trash, but not just any trailer trash. We were Vulcan."

The words seemed to catch Roland on the back of the neck, because that's what he started rubbing, rubbing hard. His drink was finished, and he turned the glass upside down the way he did when he was little and it was milk. *All gone*, he would say. He was always so proud of that. *All gone.*

"How come you never talk about it, Dad? All the other winners, that's all they do, brag about it for the rest of their lives like Mr. Zumbado and Father Rob. I've never heard you say anything about it, not even the slightest detail."

"It was a long time ago."

"People stop me all the time, tell me 'You should have seen your dad the year he won, he was absolutely unstoppable.' They say more than that, too. They say you never cheated, never turned on anyone, didn't bother with ambushes. It was like all that was beneath you and you enjoyed being the underdog. Twenty to one, thirty to one. You didn't sweat the odds, shot every last one of them to gain the finals. They talk about the day you won, how you faced off against Randy Fox on Main Street and shot him right in the heart."

"Fox hunting. He was foxy, but I outfoxed him."

He didn't smile, my humorless son.

"You and Mom when I was born? You wanted a girl, didn't you? I know that's the way it works, that moms want daughters, but aren't dads supposed to want sons?"

"Years ago they did," I mumbled.

"You know it as well as I do, Dad. I've never been good at anything—it's always the other kids who are good. This is my one and only chance, winning. I've never lived up to your expectations, not even close, but I feel I can now. You've always told me I need confidence, belief in myself, and now for the first time I understand what you mean. All I need is a little help and I can pull it off."

Help? He didn't elaborate, went instead to the door to make sure it was double locked. I followed him upstairs, sat on his bed, told him what I had to tell him. Advice on what kind of gun to use. Tips on recognizing danger. How you can stay just out of range of your opponent, then, when their ammunition runs dry, move in for the kill. Was that the kind of help he was looking for? He nodded at everything I said, but seemed more interested in his phone.

Some of it must have sunk in. As March turned to April, he started off on a rampage that brought him up with the leaders. He was ruthless enough to plug Trevor Limbaugh in the back at a frozen yogurt shop, which allowed him to form a new alliance with Ravi O'Reilly whose father is in stocks. The two of them stole a cherry picker from a construction site, drove it to Carla and Davida Walton's house, the twins who are the prettiest girls in class. It's wonderfully secure, with a high hedge around it, alarm systems, a razor wire fence—but that's what the cherry picker was for. It brought them well above the defenses, and there right below them, sunbathing naked by the pool, were the twins. An easy shot—a whitewater shot we call this—and the shock of it, the utter surprise, cascaded the girls over into the water where they floated face down, their bottoms pink as beach balls.

There was some trouble over the cherry picker, but I called Ravi's dad and between the two of us we managed to smooth it over.

We have a leader board to track results—two boards actually, one at the high school and a bigger one downtown. Roland was getting up there now—his was one of the five teams just below the top. I was surprised after the Bank Street incident not to see Crystal Mack's name up there as well. She was there, but a good six or seven places down, and when I studied the board closer I saw she hadn't registered a kill in the last two weeks.

Had she gotten discouraged? Were the odds too long, for a person of her background? Maybe she worked after school, didn't have time? Did her friends make fun of her for getting involved with the rich kids? Was her deadbeat dad causing trouble? It's odd, I can't really explain, but I felt disappointed about that, her having to give up.

I've told you how I spend my Monday lunch hours. On Tuesdays, I go to Rotary. On Wednesday, it's political committee work. Thursdays I volunteer at the elementary school reading to third-graders. Fridays I get some exercise in before the weekend.

I always run the same loop—out from downtown past the railroad yards underneath the interstate to where the factories used to be. The interstate sits up on pylons and underneath is always dark. The rumble of traffic makes the paint fleck off, and when I emerge back in the sunlight I stop and dust the scabs from my shoulders. There's a small park there, or at least the ghost of a park, with a cement picnic table, a rusty seesaw, and a pathetic set of swings.

I'd never seen anyone there, not even homeless, but this time I noticed someone watching me from the table, a shape gridded up in shadows from the remains of the chain-link fence. *Her again*, I remember thinking, though at first it wasn't any more definite than that. She had her head bowed down like she was praying to the cement, but when she saw me she sat up straight, gave me a look that was nine parts scowl.

You're probably ahead of me on guessing—yes, it was Crystal Mack. I went over to her, made my expression as friendly as I could. Pioneers, encountering Indians when our town was first settled, must have approached them the same way, half-afraid they would bolt, half-afraid they wouldn't.

"You should try the swings," I said, making my voice as gentle as I could.

She frowned, shook her head the bare minimum to register as a no.

"I don't like swings. Swings scare me."

She wore a black hooded sweatshirt, but now, with the same brazen, don't-give-a-damn gesture I'd seen at the grill, she reached behind her back and tugged it off. *Here, look at these if you want to look*—it was like someone exposing herself, so part of me wanted to laugh. So vulgar! So innocent! She had on a t-shirt from a rock band, but of course that's not what I was meant to look at. Some girls have breasts that make you ache to put your hands around them and squeeze, and others have breasts you long to rest your head on and weep, but never until her had I seen a girl whose breasts made you want to do both.

"You're Crystal," I said, as paternally as I could. "I saw you at the Grill, what you did there. Nice work, very professional."

Her red hair looked curlier than it had in the restaurant—painfully curled, to the point I wanted to dig my fingers in the tangles and start untwisting. And her neck! Her tattoo was so poorly done I was tempted to spit on it, smudge it out with my hand. She had delicate blue veins, but the tattoo seemed to mock them by being so much bluer.

Other than that? Her face was a strong one, not just in character but in sheer tensile strength. Her eyelids looked like they lifted weights, her cheeks like they did pushups—the only vulnerable part of her were her full, pouty-looking lips. There were dabs of peach-colored lipstick on the corners, but only dabs, as if she had snuck some on in a department store, then run out when the clerk started yelling.

"Not much of a park, huh? I don't blame you about the swings. They're awfully rusty."

She didn't respond to that, nor to my next equally well-intentioned remarks. I was just about to give up and resume running when she said something that made me stop.

"I know you."

"You know me?"

"You're one of them."

I stared at her—no, beyond her. The park is just high enough it commands a view of downtown across the river. We don't have many tall buildings, but they shone brilliantly in the April sunshine like they had been scrubbed and polished for spring. Was that why she came there? To stare at the beauty of it, the promise? Diamonds, planted in rows, wouldn't have looked so close, so graspable.

"Yes, I suppose I am," I said.

And that was about it, as far as our conversation went. Nothing was going to get her to look at me.

"Well, good luck," I said. "May the best person win."

"Yeah," she mumbled. "Right. Lucky me."

"I mean that. You deserve a lot of credit."

She tried smiling—was it meant to be flirty?

"You know where to find me now," she said.

But it was sad, not flirty. She said it like the game was up.

I was back to the road, about to resume my run, when I heard a yell.

"Hey mister!"

She was standing up on the picnic table, her shirt billowing in the breeze, her hands cupped around her mouth to make sure I heard.

"You have an asshole for a son!"

Next day Crystal came out firing. By infiltrating a McDonald's, putting on their cap, bribing the window girl, she managed to shoot a vanload of cheerleaders, waiting until they rolled down the windows to accept their fries. A. J. Morgan was considered one of the favorites, but she gunned him down inside a head shop where he'd gone to buy rolling paper, never suspecting anyone knew he went there. She resumed her favorite disguise, an unwed mother pushing a stroller, and shot Connor Jones in the back a moment before he was going to shoot Kelly Dow in her back—and then, stepping over Connor on the pavement, she shot Kelly, too.

Her next assassination was the most controversial. She put on blackface, pretended she was cleaning toilets in the convenience store out on the state highway. Again, the Crystal touch—blending in with people no one sees. She hosed George Lehmann that way, probably her most dangerous remaining opponent, and everyone was up in arms, white and blacks both, with all kinds of nasty things being said about racism.

Roland, to give him credit, wasn't pissed about the blackface business. He was already so pissed at her he couldn't be more pissed, no matter what she did.

"The slut! The whore! Who does she think she is!"

We were back on the couch again—it had become his headquarters, the place he came to bitch and moan.

"That phony act she puts on. I'm so discriminated against, I'm so disadvantaged. I mean, get a life! She's a taker, not a maker."

He leaned forward toward the coffee table, stared at me with great intensity, though not enough to hide the self-pity.

"This is my chance, do you understand that? Three people left beside me, now that I finished off Ravi. Three people! It's all going to be decided in the next three days."

Next morning, driving out to Zumbado's mall project, a sudden impulse made me get off at Exit Nine. This was the old Rodeo neighborhood, though no one ever knew why it was called that, other than how wild it got on paycheck night. Not much of this is left—nothing really. It's a development now, Purling Acres, and I arranged the financing myself.

I parked opposite the gatehouse. The security guards squinted over at me, and I saw one of them reach for binoculars, but when you drive the kind of car I drive you're never considered suspicious.

There weren't many signs of life, even though it was Saturday. Too hot probably—we'd had record high temperatures three days in a row. A young family walked their golden retriever along the perimeter fence, and they looked happy enough, the little blond girl in particular. She was a charmer—she kept skipping to catch up with her parents—and that made me feel good, since you never see anyone skipping anymore. I watched them until they vanished behind the first row of condos.

The tenements are gone, the stench of the factory whose shadow sat across our roof. And yet it was easier than you might think to summon it back again, what I felt the year I was Roland's age, walking the alleys, pacing the streets. When I was little, I always felt hunted. I don't mean the way a deer is hunted, by men carrying rifles, but like there were forces out to get me I couldn't identify, let alone escape. Instead of bullets, they fired food stamps and uncles drunk on Ripple and thrift-store clothing that reeked of all the bodies that had worn them before you and mothers who had to be bailed out after shoplifting and fathers who spent all day stoned in front of the TV and the angry look people gave you like it was all your fault.

But then suddenly it ended—at seventeen, between one day and the day, I found a hardness in myself I could use to shoot my way to the top. Without Assassins, I might never have known that—the adrenaline rush of stalking someone who stalks you, the jump in status, the great leveling, that comes with pulling the trigger. Hunted into hunter. Isn't that still the greatest transformation a young person can make?

It had carried me a long way in life. A long way. And yet why was I sensing it again, the feeling that the tables had been turned for a second time, and once again it was me who was being stalked?

*You're getting old*, I told myself. I glanced in the mirror, wished I hadn't.

I was just about to go when the security guard, who had never left off eyeing me, came over on his scooter for a closer look.

"Mr. Adams!" he said, when I rolled down the window. "Didn't recognize you. Sorry about that, sir."

"No problem, Hank."

"Hey, that boy of yours? The whole town's rooting for him. Better him than that tramp! Wish him well for us, will you? A natural born predator, just like his dad."

We were entering crunch time, the second week of April, when something totally unexpected happened that turned the entire competition on its head.

There were four left standing. Roland Adams, Crystal Mack, Eric Price, Teresa Koch. Teresa had gotten into Princeton, so you would think she'd have nothing to worry about. Eric wasn't bothering with college—he had launched a computer start-up with my bank's help. Both had remained pretty nonchalant about their shooting, but just because of that they'd done very well. Waterproof is the term we use. Nothing could touch them.

But yesterday that changed. They couldn't handle the pressure and scrutiny that came with being semifinalists— either that, or maybe they just didn't give a damn anymore. During lunch hour, they exited school together carrying their weapons. Were they having a shootout, people wondered, an old-fashioned duel? Everyone, students and teachers alike, crowded to the windows to watch. Eric and Teresa crossed the street so they were off school property, sat down facing each other on the sidewalk, solemnly shook hands, then simultaneously shot each other in the heart.

So now only Roland and Crystal are left—and you could have won big money betting on them being our finalists. The school, the town, are solidly on Roland's side, but this hasn't increased his self-confidence.

"It isn't fair!" he keeps saying, like he's been saying it

since he was seven. "No one knows where she lives, where she hangs out. She doesn't bother coming to school anymore. She's little more than a dropout, and why should dropouts be allowed to play?"

His buddies have organized a bodyguard to keep him protected—he doesn't go anywhere without football players huddled around him as a wall. He had scouts out searching for her, combing the bad parts of town. And yet the only place he feels safe, absolutely safe, is upstairs in his bedroom. That's where he is right now—upstairs in his room with his computers and phones linking him to his scouts. Tomorrow is the final day of the competition, and if he doesn't shoot her or she doesn't shoot him, then they face off at Main Street at noon on Saturday.

"I need to get some sleep," he said, stumbling past me in the hall. Then, catching my look, "It's not fair, I'm telling you! How can you shoot a ghost you can't find? Where is she? Where in hell is she?"

I felt like hurling something at him. Be a man!—that's what I felt like hurling. The house reeked of cowardice and self-pity, and I had to get away from it. I grabbed my jacket, went out to the car, started driving without any fixed direction. Darkness, motion—surely these would calm me down. But I was fooling myself, because I did have a direction, though right to the last moment I pretended otherwise.

The stamp-sized park under the interstate, the forgotten park that was Crystal's hiding place and probably her home. I pulled off the road over flattened beer cans and shattered bottles, turned the engine off, sat and stared. The light up on the highway spilled over in purple sheets just strong enough to coat the seesaw, table, and swings in a mottled light, so it made them look like ornaments placed on the bottom of an aquarium to give guppies a place to hide.

I got out of the car, buttoned up my jacket, started walking. There was no sign of anyone, but then, just as I came to the cement picnic table, Crystal stepped out of the shadows directly in my path. Making sure I was alone—who could blame her? She was dressed like a little girl—no, a whore. A whore dressed like a schoolgirl to tantalize her clients. Bow in hair, prim white blouse, short plaid skirt—all that was missing was the lollipop. Her latest disguise, and it seemed to suit her, like she was finally dressed as herself.

"Hey," she said, very softly.

She acted sure of herself, confident. She had lost weight since last time, and something was different about her expression. It was more business-like, more of a mask. Her lipstick was professionally applied—her hair looked done by a stylist. She was this close to success now—this close!—and she was readying her body and face so no one could ever underestimate her again.

"I knew you'd come," she said.

She walked right over to me, stopped only when her breasts touched my shirt, looked up at me in a way there could be no mistaking.

"Where is he?" she asked, in a husky whisper. She brought her hands up to her blouse, toyed with the buttons, unfastened the first one, then the second, looked up to watch me watching.

Our eyes met—and simple as that we had our deal, and we both knew it was a deal, both understood its terms. She slid her hands down my hips as a guide to lower herself until she knelt directly in front of me. She smiled again, made sure I saw her smiling, reached for my jacket and separated it until there was nothing between her mouth and my pants.

"Get up."

She didn't hear me, not at first. I dug my hands into her curls, and she read that wrong, moved in closer.

"Get up, Crystal. Go over to the swings."

That got her up all right. She stared at me like I had said something horribly perverted, something she hadn't expected in her worst nightmares.

"Swings!" I said, brutally this time.

I grabbed her arm, so she had no choice but to stumble across the dirt with me. The swings looked like gallows, but the chains were still intact and so were the seats. I pulled her around until her bottom was up against the metal slat, then shoved her down until she was sitting. I couldn't see her face, but I could feel the fear spasm through her shoulders. "I'm afraid of swings," she told me last time—but what kind of girl is afraid of swings?

"This won't hurt," I said, but it did nothing to calm her. The chains creaked as they took her weight, then creaked even louder as I pushed her forward. She acted like she had never been on swings before, didn't know she was supposed to put her hands up on the chain and hold on. I had to show her, closing her fingers around the rust until she understood. She held on tight after that. She held on like the links were throats she had to choke before they choked her.

I pushed harder, more firmly each time—up, down, back, forth—until she was going high enough her legs were up above her head and she had no choice but to lean back, which gave her more momentum, making the arc even more extreme. I held my hands out as a cushion—her shoulders, hitting them, would start her forward again—and the contact was just long enough, firm enough, I could gauge her reaction.

It was all fear at first—never, touching a woman, had I felt such tension. I wanted her to laugh, giggle, kick her feet in delight, and then, when I realized I wasn't going to get that, wanted only for her to relax and trust me—to feel that in her shoulders, one sweet moment of total surrender, total trust.

*Up, down. Back, forth. In, out. Up, down. . . .*

The swing squealed like mice being throttled. Like iron being fed into a shredder. Like rust trying to sing.

I pushed her a final time, then stepped away, stood in a muddy spot near the bars until her momentum gradually stopped. She slid off the seat, brushed the hair out of her eyes, reached under her miniskirt to scratch her bottom, then stared at me in what could have been triumph but could merely have been the expectancy of being paid.

I felt guilty now, ashamed, soiled. All I wanted was to get away from her—but a deal is a deal.

"He's sleeping in his room. I'll tell the guard at the gate that he's expecting a friend—you won't have any problem. The porch light will be on and I'll unlock the door. His bedroom is at the top of the stairs, the first one on the right. He's been taking Benadryl to sleep, so you won't have any problem there either. Understand?"

She nodded like a little girl trusting her father, hanging on every word—but it was too late for that, and it didn't do anything to improve my mood.

"Good luck," I mumbled. And maybe that was the worst thing I did to her, or the second worst. Wishing her luck just when it ran out.

I didn't tell her about the rest of my plan—I've only formulated it this minute, driving back home in the car. I admire grit and determination, know how far it can take you, but times have changed now, and it's a different world than the one we grew up in. Reality is reality—I can only bow to that, no matter my personal leanings. And so I will slap Roland awake when I get home, explain in a few quick sentences what's up, tell him to wait for her in the shadows below the stairs.

"Aim for the boobs," I'll tell him, so there's no chance he'll miss. "I'm handing you Crystal on a silver platter," though, like the rest of this town, he's never shown much appreciation for my puns.

CPSIA information can be obtained
at www.ICGtesting.com
Printed in the USA
LVHW05s1100260918
591366LV00006B/6/P

9 780997 452884